D0856937

High Midnight

A Toby Peters Mystery

High Midnight

Stuart Kaminsky

St. Martin's Press
New York

For information, write: St. Martin's Press,
175 Fifth Avenue, New York, N.Y. 10010
Manufactured in the United States of America

Library of Congress Cataloging in Publication Data

Kaminsky, Stuart M
High midnight.

I. Title
PS3561.A43H5 813'.54 80-29121
ISBN 0-312-37234-5

Design by Manuela Paul

10 9 8 7 6 5 4 3 2 1

First Edition

This one is for Marcus Parry

High Midnight

CHAPTER ONE

Two sailors had thrown Jack Ellis into the elevator shaft on the eighth floor of the Ocean Palms Hotel. If the elevator hadn't been on the way up from the sixth floor at the time, Jack would have been a short order of ground house detective. As it was, he wound up with a right kneecap that reminded a sentimental surgeon at Los Angeles County Hospital of the thousand-piece jigsaw puzzle of Niagara Falls his mother had given him for his tenth birthday.

The two sailors, whom Jack had interrupted while they were dancing on a shoe-polish salesman from Sioux Falls, Iowa, had been scolded severely and sent back to duty on the U.S.S. *Wasp.* Sailors were top-priority items in 1942 and broken-down house detectives two for a mercury dime.

Before delirium set in Jack called me to ask if I wanted to fill in for him at the Ocean Palms till he was back on whatever they could construct to keep him reasonably balanced when he went unpatriotically after his next battalion of servicemen having a good time. Jack had been a security guard at Warner Brothers until about a year ago. I had been a guard at the studio a few years before him. We had similar backgrounds right down to being fired personally by Jack Warner. When I separated Jack's words from the groans, I told him that I'd be at the Ocean Palms that night. He said thanks and passed out. I heard the phone bounce away on the tile floor and a nurse shout, "Shit."

So for three weeks I was acting house dick at the Ocean Palms on Main in downtown Los Angeles, a few blocks from my own office on Hoover and Ninth. My office was in the Farraday Building, which had seen much better days, but the Ocean Palms had not. The hotel went up in 1912 without high hopes and had managed, with the help of time, earthquakes and transients of uncertain ilk, to remain on the short side of respectability. The hotel had worn away a few dozen managers, a house staff of hundreds and as many house detectives as there were slaves who built the great pyramid.

The Ocean Palms keys to success were the war, proximity to the Greyhound bus terminal and low prices without pride. Soldiers, sailors and marines on passes checked into rooms and went out into halls looking for trouble. Small-town kids who wanted to break into the movies checked in and met sailors in halls looking for trouble. Salesmen with low budgets and prostitutes on the way down but not quite out roamed and met each other. The hotel got its twenty-five bucks' worth from me for three weeks until that cold Monday, February 16, 1942. The temperature had dropped to the thirties in Los Angeles. I heard it was 22 in San Gabriel.

It was noon when I walked into the Ocean Palms lobby, wearing one of my two suits and a topcoat that had been in and out of hock to Hy O'Brien of O'Brien's Clothes for Him so many times that Hy and I considered it community property. There was rain in the air, which threatened my bad back, and the news was rotten. Singapore had fallen to the Japanese. Burma and Sumatra were on the way out. Eleanor Roosevelt said women should register for the draft. Japanese enemy aliens and their American-born sons and daughters had till the following Sunday to remove themselves from restricted areas, meaning if you even looked Oriental you had six days to get out of Los Angeles. The news stunk and so did I. I had been sleeping days and working nights and bathing not at all.

When I entered the lobby, two men in coats were leaning against the registration desk. I recognized one of them and knew that as bad as the news was for the United States, it was going to get worse for me personally.

"Peters," said the shorter of the two, standing up with both hands in his pockets.

I had never known his name, but I knew his job. I had run into him in Chicago a year earlier when I was on a case. He looked a lot like Lou Costello but he worked for Frank Nitti, which didn't make him funny at all. He had tried to kill me once and saved my life once and had ordered me permanently out of Chicago. Maybe now Nitti had decided that the United States wasn't big enough for the two of us. The other guy in the lobby, a massive creature with a worried look, was dressed like a looming shadow of Costello. They both wore dark hats and coats. Both had their hands in their pockets. They could have gone on the stage and done a dance.

It was too late for me to run, and I was too easy to find if I did. Besides, this was my territory and I wasn't about to give it up without finding out why.

"How'd you like to take a ride with us?" the bigger one said in a voice that would have knocked over the palms in the lobby if they had not all been stolen years earlier. The big one moved toward me.

"A ride would be very nice," I said. "Mind if I tell. . . ."

"We told the manager it was an emergency," said Costello. "He was very understanding."

"Don't get funny," the big guy said, bringing up the rear as we went back outside.

"I'll try to keep a straight face," I said.

Their car was a big black '39 Packard with California plates. I got in the back with Costello, who pulled out his .45 and dug it into my stomach, searching for a reasonable place to drill an extra navel. The big man drove.

"Palm trees, will you look at that, right on the street? Will you look at that?" said Costello.

I looked out the window at the palm trees I had seen almost every day of my forty-five years on this planet.

"Palm trees," I repeated.

Costello had one of those dark, weatherbeaten faces mass-produced by the grit of cities. He was tough, thick and compact.

"Marco and me been in Los Angeles four, five hours, that's all," Costello said, leaning toward me and nodding at the driver.

"You sure you got the right guy?" I tried.

Costello grinned. "I know you, Peters." He pushed the gun even further into my stomach and then leaned back to admire the palms.

"You going to tell me what's going on?" I said. "Or did you just pick me up to show you the sights and admire your taste in palm trees?"

The grin left Costello's face. "I don't like jokers. You remember that? Marco don't like jokers either, and we don't like bright boys either, do we, Marco?"

Marco's huge shoulders shrugged.

"Look what you did," Costello sighed. "You almost ruined our first morning in Los Angeles."

"Sorry," I said. "But you're not making this an Ovaltine day for me either. Where are we going?"

"Santa Monica," rumbled Marco from the front seat in a voice that suggested a botched ghetto tonsillectomy and gangster movies.

"You tell him nothing," hissed Costello. "Nothing. Nothing."

"What's the difference?" rasped Marco. "He'll see when

we get there. He's certainly familiar with the environment."

Costello sat back to whisper to me and worked the gun barrel around to my kidney. "Marco's building his vocabulary," he sneered softly. *"Reader's Digest.* Thinks it'll make a difference."

"How many mugs back in Chicago you know can use a word like 'environment'?" Marco said.

"He's got a point," I said.

"Be quiet, bright boy," Costello whispered.

"I don't think I was ever a boy," I said. "I never had time to be a boy. And I'm not going to start being one now."

"Make you feel better to say that?" sighed Costello. "You feel brave now? Huh."

I shrugged, and he gave three quick jabs to my kidney with the gun barrel.

He smiled, and I tried to smile back. He held a fat, dark finger to his lips and said, "Shhh."

We drove for fifteen minutes in silence except for the traffic outside and the pinging of a light, cold rain. I cleared my throat. Costello pressed the gun into my sore kidney.

"I don't want to hear you breathe," he said.

"Which Santa Monica are we going to?" I said softly.

"Joke again?" he hissed. "What did I say about jokes?" He punctuated each word with a sharp jab. I groaned.

"Is there a plethora of Santa Monicas?" Marco asked, over the engine and my groaning.

"I only know one and it's not in Nevada," I said. "You're heading east."

Marco hit the brakes, sending us into a skid. We slid sideways into a muddy hill and stopped. Marco turned his thick, round head to face us over the seat. The rain streaming down the windows cast dark, quivering lines on his face. He did not look happy. He did not look angry, either. What I saw in that massive face and black eyes was a dangerous fear.

"I told you we shouldn't have come here," he said. "We

don't know this place. Things are going wrong already. It's going to be calamitous."

Costello looked at Marco's frightened face and then past him out the window. "The Japs are not going to land here and they're not going to bomb Los Angeles. We just do our job and get out and nothing is going to happen."

Marco's eyes met mine and then turned dangerously to Costello. "Who said anything about bombs?" he said. He pointed a massive finger at himself. "I ask you. Did I say anything about bombs?" His hand moved inside his coat.

"Crap," sighed Costello, looking out the window at the passing traffic. "You're just scared. I know what you're scared of. I listened to you for ten hours on that plane."

"You shouldn't denunciate me in front of strangers," Marco said dangerously.

"Shut up and drive out of here, or brother-in-law or no brother-in-law, you're going to be through when we get back to Chicago," Costello said.

I could see by Marco's eyes that this was the wrong tack. "I don't think the Japanese are going to land here or bomb," I said evenly.

"See," said Costello.

"On the other hand," I said almost to myself, "we are due for a major earthquake."

"I don't like it," Marco said, looking out the back window for enemy Zeroes.

"We had no choice," Costello said, looking at me. "He told us . . ."

"We could have declined," answered Marco. "We could have procrastinated."

"Talk English and drive," said Costello, taking the gun from my kidney and bringing it in front of him in the general direction of massive Marco, who was, if nothing else, an easy target at this or any distance up to a hundred yards. Rain shadows did a mocking dance on Marco's frightened face.

He took off his hat to pat a sweating bald head. Then his fear turned to anger. A gun pointed at him was something he understood.

"I don't like where that gun is pointing," Marco croaked.

And I didn't like the whole damned conversation. In a few seconds I could be sprayed all over the backseat, the innocent victim of crossfire between two feebleminded refugees from a remake of *Scarface.*

"I'll tell you how to get to Santa Monica," I said. "I know a shortcut." I was in desperate need of a more sane level of kidnapper.

"Roosevelt ain't so sure they won't bomb," Marco went on, staring at Costello. "If he is sure, why's he want to move the factories East? And what about this earthquake stuff?"

"Politics," said Costello.

"Just turn the car around and go back on this street," I tried.

Marco and Costello were eye to eye.

"Palm trees all the way," I said. It had no effect, so I tried, "Isn't someone waiting for us?"

That moved them. Costello nodded, and Marco turned around. The gun found its way back into the nook it had carved in my kidney.

"Politics has nothing to do with it," Marco said, turning the car around and almost causing a collision with a truck. "Politics are irrelevant to the situation."

Nothing much more happened on the way to Santa Monica. We did stop for tacos and Pepsi at a stand I like. Marco went in while Costello and I peered through the drizzle in search of palms.

"I don't see the damned mountains," Costello grumbled.

"When the sky clears, you'll see them, and we'll go through some in a few minutes."

Marco ate five tacos and I ate two. Costello wanted me to pay for my own but we couldn't get the bill straight, so Marco said it was on him. He asked a few questions about earthquakes and we continued on our pilgrimage, three buddies out for a lark on a Monday afternoon.

It was almost two in the afternoon when we got where we were going. The rain had stopped, but the sky was dark, and disgruntled thunder rumbled over the ocean a few blocks away. We were in the parking lot of a new low white brick building, a one-story affair with a few construction company trucks still around to provide finishing touches. Costello led the way through construction rubble and into the building through a double wooden door marked Delivery Entrance.

Marco breathed tabasco sauce on my neck as we moved into the damp half-light. The lights hadn't been installed yet, and the building had that new smell of mud and clay with a touch of garlic. Something moved in the corner, and three men stepped forward from the shadows of the broad room we were in. A boom of thunder shook the walls.

"You do a little sightseeing on the way?" said the man in the lead, with a slight accent I couldn't place. He was about fifty, with thin, dark hair and a mottled complexion. He was wearing a clean white smock and had his hands in his pockets like a doctor approaching a troublesome patient. The two men behind him were also wearing white smocks and serious scowls. One of them carried a large plate.

The guy with the bad complexion stepped forward and looked at me. I seemed to be what he expected. I'm about five foot nine, weigh about 160 and have a nose smashed flat by fists and fate. I look as if I've seen it all and it has seen and danced on me.

"Mr. Lombardi . . ." Marco began with what was probably going to be an apology, but Lombardi cut him off with a stare and clenched teeth that made it clear Marco had made a mistake in using his name. He held the glare for about ten seconds and then held up his left hand. One of the two guys in white, the one with the plate, stepped forward. I was sure there would be a dagger on the plate and I was about to be dispatched, with Marco following me in a matter of seconds.

"Try this," said Lombardi. He took the plate from the guy on his left and held it out to me. There were slices of pastrami, corned beef and salami and something else on it. I reached for the salami and took a bite.

"Well?" said Lombardi.

I looked around at Costello and Marco and the two guys in white while I chewed. They were all looking at me.

"Good," I said.

"Just good?" said Lombardi. "Try the pastrami and the tongue."

I tried the pastrami.

"Very good," I said. This guy had gone through a lot to get my approval of some cold cuts, and he didn't seem like the type who would respond well to criticism. I finished the pieces of meat and accepted the offer of a slice of pickled cow's tongue. I don't know how it tasted. It was a little hard to taste anything with Lombardi's face inches from mine, his right eyebrow up, his tongue a little out, waiting for my reaction.

I smiled and nodded in appreciation as I gulped down the tongue slice.

"See," grinned Lombardi, "a native likes it."

We were pals now. He put his right arm over my shoulder and led me into a corner away from the others.

"I got this idea back East," he whispered into my ear. "A guy I know said the delicatessen in Los Angeles was awful, couldn't get a decent pastrami, no smoked fish, lox, nothing. So about a year ago I decided to move out here, semi-retire, open a kosher-style factory."

"Kosher-style?" I asked sweetly.

Lombardi nodded and pointed back at the guy in white who had held the platter of meat. "Stevie's old lady was Jewish. Stevie will manage the factory."

"Oh," I said as we walked in a little circle, Lombardi's arm getting heavier on my shoulder. "And how do I–"

"You see," Lombardi went on, pausing only to touch a shiny new slicing machine delicately, "there are maybe a couple thousand, maybe more, restaurants in LA that should be carrying my line. With my two imported salesmen from Chicago and my own men, we should be able to convince most of them to take a good supply each and every day. You agree?" I agreed.

"Good," he went on with a wink. "Now this can run into big money–not as big as some other things I could have gone into, but this is a labor of love, you know what I mean?"

"A labor of love," I agreed, wanting to shift his arm from my shoulder.

"But," he said, stopping suddenly and gripping my shoulder, "there is a problem."

"A problem," I repeated, since repeating seemed to be getting me into the least trouble.

"A problem," he nodded sadly. "Someone is stirring into things I don't want stirred into, things from a long time ago that could embarrass a friend of mine, maybe cause trouble for my business. We don't want trouble for my business, do we?"

"We do not," I said emphatically.

Lombardi bit his lower lip and did some more nodding. I was saying the right thing. He gave me a playful punch on the shoulder.

"Good, good," he whispered. "I knew we could get along. Now all you have to do is string a certain client of yours along for a week or two and then tell him that there's nothing to worry about and that you advise him to do what a certain producer wants done. You know what to say."

"I do?"

The friendly look began to fade from Lombardi's face, and he looked at Marco and Costello.

"You do," he said.

"I haven't got a client," I said. "Haven't had one for months. I'm filling in as house dick at the . . ."

Lombardi's finger had gone up to his lips and touched them, a signal I took for me to shut up.

"You know," he said, "I was not the nicest kid on my block when I was a kid. I have a bad temper."

"You?"

"Yes," he said with a shrug. "It's hard to believe, but it's true, and sometimes I get crazy ideas." His free hand went up to his head to show me that the ideas came from there and not from a lower region. "Like I wonder what hot dogs would taste like if they were mixed with meat and bones from the right hand of a private detective. You ever wonder things like that?"

I couldn't get any words out, but I shook my head slowly to indicate that my curiosity never went in that direction.

"Well," Lombardi continued, "you go have a talk with Mr. Cooper . . ."

"Cooper?" I said.

"Cooper," he repeated as if I were feebleminded.

"Are you sure you have the right private detective?" I tried.

"Your name is Toby Peters. Office on Hoover?"

"Right."

"You're the right one."

"Right. I'm to talk to Cooper. Tell him there is nothing I can find. Tell him he should do what the producer wants."

"You've got it," said Lombardi, "and be sure my name and our little visit don't come up in the conversation."

We had marched around the big room with our conversation punctuated by thunder, rain and one loud, nervous taco burp from Marco. We were back where we started, with the guys in white on one side and Marco and Costello behind me.

"Mind telling me which Cooper?" I said.

"You are joking," said Lombardi. "I can appreciate a sense of humor. Our friends from Chicago, they don't have much sense of humor, and they're going to be keeping an eye on you for a while, just to be sure you understand our deal. Here, I got a little something to remember me by."

The other guy in white stepped forward, his hands behind his back. I tightened my stomach muscles and pursed my lips to protect my teeth from whatever he was going to hit me with. His right hand came out with a brown paper bag.

Lombardi took the bag and handed it to me. "Assortment of cold cuts. Take them. Enjoy them. And do what we agreed. Remember my crazy ideas."

"Hot dogs," I said.

"You got it," he grinned, releasing my shoulder. "I hope I don't see you again, Mr. Peters."

What do you say to that kind of parting line? I turned, brown paper bag in my hand. Marco and Costello took their places at my side and walked me toward the door. Behind us I could hear Lombardi's voice getting back to business, talking kosher-style bologna and expansion into the West Coast lox box market.

The rain had stopped. It was still dark, but the black clouds were drifting inland fast.

"Did you hear what he said?" Marco groaned. "He wants us to stay around here and sell salami."

"Salami, beer," Costello said with a shrug to show it was all the same to him, all the while prodding me into the backseat of the car. Marco got into the driver's seat, grumbling.

"Where you want us to take you?" Costello said. His gun remained in his shoulder holster. For him, the whole thing was over. He had only a few more lines to deliver.

I told them to take me back to the Ocean Palms. This time I gave directions right away, and we were back there in twenty minutes.

As I got out, still clutching my now grease stained brown bag, Costello delivered his line. "You want to keep breathing this wet air, you do what you were told. We're gonna keep an eye on you. Right, Marco?"

Marco neither turned nor responded. His mind was filled with images of Japanese soldiers on *banzai* charges down La Cienega or cracks suddenly opening in the ground on Sunset. I went into the Ocean Palms and was greeted by the manager, James R. Schwoch, a thin guy with bug eyes, nervous hands and a frequent glance over his shoulder for eavesdroppers. He wore the same brown suit and tie he had worn since I met him.

"Where have you been?" he demanded.

"I was kidnapped by the new cold cut king of Santa Monica," I explained.

Schwoch sneered.

"Get up to 212. Someone tried to commit suicide."

The someone was an eighteen-year-old girl from Eau Claire, Wisconsin, whose money had run out with her new boyfriend. She didn't want any of my pastrami, but I got her to accept twenty bucks, almost a week's pay, for a bus ticket back home. She thanked me and I told her that no one had ever really killed herself on eighteen aspirin. She said that was all she could afford. She had considered cutting her wrists or jumping out the window, but her imagination was too good. When I got her packed, I used the phone in her room to call Jack Ellis.

"How's the leg?" I asked.

"Cast up to my ass, but I can walk," he said. "Goddamn thing is driving me nuts. I can't read, can't listen to the radio. All I can do is think about how much it itches."

"Can you come back to work?"

"I don't know," he said slowly. "It'd take my mind off the itching. What's up?"

I sketched it out and told him it would only take me a few days, but if he couldn't make it back I'd get someone else to fill in.

"No," Ellis said. "Maybe I can get a chance to kick a few sailors with this cast."

"That's unpatriotic. There's a war going on."

"Right," he said. "Between me and the US armed forces. I'll get my wife to drive me down. You can take off."

I tried to get the twenty bucks back from Schwoch but he wasn't having any. It had been my idea to give the girl the money, not his. I told him Ellis was coming back, and he liked the idea. I wondered if he would give Ellis the hotel manager's equivalent of the purple heart, but I didn't wait around to see. I didn't know how long my brown paper bag would hold up, and I had some thinking to do.

My '34 Buick had recently been painted a straight dark blue by No-neck Arnie, the mechanic on Eleventh. The paint was already bubbling. I had sixty bucks and a problem. The immediate problem was the stain on the seat next to me being made by the Lombardi kosher-style cold cuts. The next problem was a client I supposedly had named Cooper. I turned on the car radio and listened to the war news for a few seconds and then turned to KFI to catch Don Winslow, who was winning the war even if we weren't.

What did I have? A client named Cooper, who had something to do with movies. Lombardi, who had recently moved to the Coast from the East and wanted to remain a noncelebrity. How many Coopers were there? Gladys Cooper, Jackie Cooper, Meriam C. Cooper, Gary Cooper. Something pinged in my head. Something about Gary Cooper. I urged it to come out. Don Winslow urged a spy to come out of a submarine, but both remained inside.

The sky was clearing but the day was still damned cold when I pulled in front of Mrs. Plaut's boarding house on Heliotrope, where I lived. Mrs. Plaut greeted me on the porch. She was somewhere in the vicinity of eighty years old, with more determination than the Russians holding Leningrad and as much hearing as a light pole. She was under the impression that I was an exterminator with connections in the movie industry. With my help, she was writing a history of her family.

"Mr. Peelers, you are home early," she said.

"Yes," I said. "I . . ."

"Yes, problems," she sighed as I came on the porch. "My father used to say this is a doggie dog world."

"Right," I said, trying to skip past her.

"I'll have another chapter by Saturday," she said, putting her bony arm out, an arm that had uncanny strength.

"Right," I said, easing past her with my brown bag held out to keep from further ruining my suit.

I did not bound up the stairs, but I went as quickly as I could. I passed my own door and knocked at Gunther's. Gunther Wherthman was my next-door neighbor and probably my best friend. Gunther, all three foot nine of him, answered immediately. He was, as always, dressed in a three-piece suit, though he worked at home translating books from German, French, Italian, Spanish, Polish and Danish into English. Gunther was Swiss. We had met on a case of mine.

"Ah, Toby," he said with reserved enthusiasm. "I have a query for you."

"Join me in my room for an early dinner," I said. "Cold cuts." I showed him the bag.

"Yes," he said. "Let me clean up first."

Gunther dirty was more clean than I would be after going through a car wash without a car. I went to my room. I had learned to appreciate the room, which was nothing like me. There was one old sofa with doilies on the arms, which I was afraid to touch, a table with three chairs, a hot plate in the corner, a sink, a small refrigerator, a few dishes and a bed with a purple blanket on which "God Bless Us Every One" had been stitched in pink by Mrs. Plaut, a painting of Abraham Lincoln and a Beech-nut gum clock on my wall received in payment from a pawnshop owner for finding his runaway grandmother. Every night I took the mattress from the bed and put it on the floor. I slept there because of a delicate back crunched in 1938 by a gentleman of the Negro persuasion, who took exception to my trying to keep him away from Mickey Rooney when I was picking up a few dollars as a guard at a premiere at Grauman's Chinese.

I took off my jacket, shoes and tie and dumped the cold cuts into a bowl. I pulled out some leftover hard rolls and a bottle of ketchup and was trying to get a dark spot off of one of my plates when Gunther came in carrying a bottle of Cresta Blanca wine and two glasses.

He put the wine on the table, examined the cold cuts, trying to hide a critical look, and made a sandwich. We drank wine and ate.

I told Gunther my adventure and asked what he thought of the food.

"While I appreciate your hospitality, Toby, I think Mr. Lombardi's cuisine could be improved."

We ate for a while longer–at least I did. Gunther finished only half a sandwich and then told me his own problem.

"I am translating what I take to be a humorous American story for an overseas broadcast. And in that story is a comic demolition company named Edifice Wrecks. I assume that is a waggish reference to Oedipus Rex. However, the joke does not translate well into Polish, and I am not adept at humor."

I could confirm that. Gunther had sat in polite amusement on several nights while I giggled at Al Pearce or Burns and Allen. I couldn't help Gunther with his problem, and he couldn't help me with mine.

"It's Gary Cooper," I said, finishing my third sandwich and downing the last of the small bottle of wine. "I know it. Something . . . Hold it. About a month ago I had a message to call Gary Cooper. Then the next day a call came canceling the message. I thought it was a joke. What if . . ."

"Someone got to Cooper saying he was you and then called telling you to cancel your call," Gunther finished.

"Right," I said. "Someone beat me out of the job."

"There could be many other explanations," said Gunther reasonably.

"Sure, but remember it's a doggie dog world out there," I said.

Gunther looked puzzled.

"I think I'll get on it right away."

Gunther volunteered to clean up. I had learned to let him. He didn't like the way I cleaned up. I didn't either.

If someone was playing Toby Peters, he had started something that could lose me a right hand. I had to deal myself in or sit around waiting for Lombardi to come and deal me out.

The first step was to find Cooper. I pulled some nickels out of my pocket and went to the pay phone in the hall. Below me I could hear Mrs. Plaut singing "I Got It Bad and That Ain't Good." She had all the words screwed up, but the melody was close.

A guy I know, a writer at *Variety* who used to do publicity at Warner Brothers, told me that Cooper was making a baseball picture for Goldwyn. He didn't know how far they were on shooting. He also said in passing that Cooper was a shoo-in for the Academy Award for *Sergeant York.* I hadn't asked him. After saying good-bye to Gunther, using the washroom down the hall and readjusting my tie, I went out in search of Gary Cooper.

CHAPTER TWO

Finding Cooper wasn't hard. Getting to him was the problem. I went to Goldwyn Studios, where I had no contacts. After I said I had an appointment with Cooper, I was told that he was on location. The guy at the gate made a phone call to the location, gave my name and after five minutes got the go-ahead from Cooper for me to come. The gate guard gave me an address in Los Angeles, and I headed for it.

Kate Smith had gotten through "Rose O'Day" on the radio when I turned the corner and parked next to an old ball park. I remembered going to a boxing match in the place when I was a kid. My old man, who never punched anyone in his life, dearly loved watching grown men go after each other in a fifteen-foot square.

I could hear voices inside the park; not the voices of crowds, but the tired voices of men at the end of a workday. A guard at the gate asked who I was and let me through. The sun was about to give up and call it a day after elbowing at the clouds without much success. The rain had stopped, but the air had a cold bite.

I walked into the stadium and saw two men out on the baseball field near first base. One was tall and lanky; the other looked chunky and older. Both of them wore baseball uniforms. I took a step toward them from behind the backstop, and a figure blocked my way.

"Where you headin', son?" came a voice I recognized but couldn't place.

"I've got an appointment with Mr. Cooper," I explained, looking up at the man before me. For a second I had the feeling that I was dreaming. I had to be. Dressed in full Yankee uniform and barring my way was Babe Ruth. The face was a little weathered and sagging, the belly a little lower than in the newsreels, the legs a bit thinner, but Babe Ruth. My mouth must have flapped open.

It stayed open when three more Yankees appeared behind Ruth. I recognized Bill Dickey by his face and Bob Meusel and Mark Koenig by their numbers.

"Why do you want to see Coop?" Dickey asked.

"I'm working for him," I explained.

Ruth nodded, and Koenig walked toward the lanky and squat guys on first base.

"Have a seat," Ruth commanded, and I sat in the first row of wooden benches. Ruth eased himself next to me, and Dickey sat on the other side. Meusel stood back a few feet, looking at me.

The question must have been on my face.

"We're making a movie," Ruth explained. "The life of Lou Gehrig. Coop is Gehrig. Lot of people been trying to get in here. They find out, pester, you know." I nodded, showing that I knew. "Some of them get unpleasant. You're not going to get unpleasant?"

"I'm not planning to be unpleasant," I said. Koenig was about fifty feet off, talking to Cooper and pointing in my direction.

"We're not shooting anything today, just getting some

publicity shots and helping Lefty teach Coop how to throw a baseball," explained Dickey.

"How to throw a baseball?" I asked.

"He can't throw," said Ruth. "Arm's been busted up from falls when he was a stunt man. Never played ball when he was a kid anyway." Ruth looked around the park and down at me. His broad face and pushed-back nose were tired reminders of what he had been.

"A few years ago after a day in the ball park I'd go out and lay one on," Ruth sighed. "Chicago, Boston, they have the best joints, even better than New York. Remember, Bill?"

"That was your game, Babe," Dickey said with a smile. His round, strong face and short blond hair under his Yankee cap made him look ready to run out on the field.

"Stomach," explained Ruth, pointing to his sagging paunch under the Yankee stripes. "Gone bad on me after all I did for it, all the good times I gave it, all the gals who admired it. Is that fair, I ask you?" Ruth winked at Dickey, who smiled politely. Koenig meanwhile was walking slowly back to us. He moved past Meusel and stood over me. I tried to rise, but he put a hand on my shoulder.

"Coop says this isn't Peters," he said.

I was about to be murdered by Murderer's Row.

"It's a mistake," I said, trying to stand again. Dickey caught my arm and pulled me down.

"Yours," said Ruth, who gripped my arm, but there was nothing much in the grip. "You think we can throw him over the fence? Can't be more than fifteen feet high. Hell, five years back I could have done it on my own."

"A mistake," I croaked as the quartet lifted me up.

They carried me toward the entrance, and I shouted over my shoulder toward Cooper. "Mr. Cooper–the threats–I know what's going on."

I didn't know what was going on, but I wanted to make

some contact with Cooper, to explain and get some answers. I dragged my feet, but the former Yankees had no trouble with me. Then, just as we hit the turnstyle, a voice behind us said, "Hold on a second."

We stopped, and I planted my feet and turned around to face Cooper and the squat man. Cooper was as big as I expected, but the touch of youthful enthusiasm he had on the screen was absent from the man. He definitely looked too old to be wearing the uniform.

"You say you were Peters or *from* Peters?" Cooper asked, pointing a long finger at me. His light eyes were unblinking.

"You've been conned, Mr. Cooper," I said rapidly. "I'm the real Peters, and I can prove it. Someone has been pretending to be me, but I know about the case. Give me a minute to prove it."

Cooper looked at me uncertainly and bit his lower lip. He looked at the Yankees for advice, but they had none to give. Ruth's stomach grumbled next to me, and everyone waited for Cooper to decide.

"Let him go, fellas, I'll give him a minute."

They let me go, and Ruth said, "You sure? You want us to stick around?"

"No," grinned Cooper, "Lefty and I can handle things here, can't we?"

"Right," said Lefty sourly.

"Keep what's left of your nose clean," Ruth told me.

"Hold it a second," I told him.

Ruth stopped, surprised.

"Can I get autographs?" I pulled a pencil and my ratty notebook out of my pocket and thrust it at him.

Ruth took them and laughed.

"You got a nerve, kid," he said and passed around the notebook for the other Yankees. I got the notebook back, and Ruth touched his cap in farewell to Cooper. I watched the four Yankees disappear under the stands, Ruth walking a little slower than the rest.

"Now talk, mister, and make it quick," said Cooper.

What I wanted to do was ask Cooper why the letters and number on his Yankee uniform were backward, but what I did was talk fast.

"Some time, maybe three weeks, four weeks ago, you called my office, asked me to call you back. I got a message the next day telling me to forget it. I'd guess someone got in touch with you, said he was Peters and took the case."

"What case?" grumbled Lefty.

"It's okay," said Cooper. "Give me a few minutes with this man, Lefty, and I'll be right back with you."

Lefty shrugged and walked back toward first base.

"From what I can piece together," I said, "someone is trying to blackmail you or threaten you into working on a film for a producer you don't want to deal with. Right so far?"

Cooper's face twisted into a pained grin, but I wasn't sure if it was because of my remarks or indigestion.

"This morning I was taken by two goons from Chicago for a ride to see a guy named Lombardi, who told me to help convince you to take the movie job."

The name Lombardi struck something in Cooper's sad eyes. He had been giving me part of his attention. Now I had all of it.

"Lombardi found the real Toby Peters–me. Threatened the real one."

"I see," said Cooper, removing his baseball cap and rubbing his sweating brow with his sleeve. With the cap off his face, he showed every one of his forty years. He looked like a man in agony.

"Then who is the man who posed as you?" Cooper asked reasonably.

"Describe him," I said.

"Maybe fifty, roly-poly sweaty fella, bald head, smokes cheap cigars . . ."

". . . and wears thick glasses that keep creeping down his nose," I finished.

"You know him," said Cooper.

"I know him and he's no private detective. He's a dentist."

"A dentist?" gulped Cooper. "I've got to admit I wasn't impressed with him, but you came recommended by a fella I know at Paramount and . . . okay. What now?"

"I'll take care of the detective-dentist," I said. "How much have you paid him?"

"Let's see, about three hundred," Cooper said, raising his forehead.

"You have a few minutes to answer some questions and tell me what's happening, and I'll take over the case."

Cooper looked puzzled, which seemed perfectly reasonable to me. He looked into my brown eyes and saw no answers. He looked into the first-baseman's glove in his left hand and saw no answers. He looked over at Lefty, who was kicking dirt behind first base, and saw no answers.

"Okay, give me a few minutes to change clothes," he finally said and then shouted at Lefty, "Let's call it a day."

Lefty waved back and walked in our direction as Cooper disappeared under the stands, walking slowly. Lefty shook his head for the entire distance from first base to my side.

"What the hell is going on here?" he asked. "How am I going to teach him how to throw with all these interruptions? Throws the ball like an old woman tossing a hot biscuit. Has a hell of a time getting his right arm over his head. We're working on it, though. He's willing enough, I'll give him that, but he doesn't know from old radiators about baseball. How can you grow up in this country and not know baseball?"

"It happens," I sympathized. "Why are the letters on his uniform reversed?"

"Gehrig was a southpaw, a first baseman," explained Lefty. "No way in the world I'm ever going to get Cooper to throw with his left hand. So some guy at Goldwyn got the idea of reversing the film so it looks as if he's throwing with the left when he's throwing with the right. That's why the letters have to be reversed. He's got uniforms both ways. He works out in them to get the feel."

"So in the movie he'll be standing at third base instead of first?"

"How the hell do I know?" Lefty growled. "The whole thing's a mistake. Cooper's a mess. He has a bad back and broken bones all over the place. He couldn't get through two innings of a real game even if he knew how to play. Gehrig played 2,130 straight games. Nobody's ever going to do that again. Hell, Cooper doesn't even look like Gehrig."

"People who go to movies don't care," I said.

"I care," said Lefty, pointing to himself. "Say, listen, Cooper is a good guy. He's trying, but this is baseball we're talking."

Five minutes later Cooper was back, but it was a different Cooper. He was wearing a body-tailored pinstripe suit, a spotlessly clean camel's hair coat and a white fedora.

"If you can give me a ride, Mr. Peters, we can talk on my way home," he said. "I'll see you tomorrow, Lefty."

Lefty said good-bye and ambled away, and I agreed to drive Cooper home.

"I didn't want to do this baseball picture," Cooper explained, getting into the Buick. I managed to slide a few napkins from my pocket under him before his camel's hair coat hit the grease spot where the cold-cut bag had been.

I pulled into the street, and he kept talking.

"Baseball's my father's game, not mine," he said softly. "About a month ago the Judge, my father, was hit by a car. He's 76."

"Sorry," I said.

"It was the Judge's idea for me to play Gehrig. My games are fast cars and good hunting, and my weakness is young ladies."

"I see," I said.

"No, you don't," he said, still softly. "When you mentioned Mr. Lombardi's name back there," he said, pointing his thumb behind us, "it reminded me of a certain young lady. She was, she said, a fan. This was back about six, seven years ago, maybe longer–a pretty blonde thing, a little on the thin side. The ones who want to get into the movies usually are. We were friendly for a few months, and then I found out she had been a friend of Lombardi's and that he was looking for her. She packed up and went, and that was the end of it."

"And now?" I urged him on.

"Now I'm interested in keeping my wife and daughter safe and getting on with my work."

"What's stopping you?"

"About a month ago, just before I called you," he said, looking out the window, "a man came up to me, tough-looking gent about your size, built like a giant brick. He gave me a list of reasons why I should make a movie for a third-rate producer-director named Max Gelhorn. That list included a reminder of Lola . . ."

"The thin blonde . . ."

"Right," said Cooper, "and a few other things which seemed much more substantial and which I'd rather not go into with you if I don't have to."

"You might have to at some point," I said.

"If it comes to that, I'll decide. Now I'd like to say I

punched out that man and laid him flat like one of the characters I play, but to tell it straight, Mr. Peters . . ."

"Toby . . ."

"Toby," he went on, "I'm no fighter. I'm an actor. I've been mended and patched up, but I have more wounds than a war veteran. My pelvis was broken when I was a kid. It never mended. I can't sit on a horse straight. I have about half my hearing. A bomb went off too close to my ear one day about ten years back when I was doing a war picture with Fay Wray. My stomach is bad, my arms are weak from too many movie falls and to put it straight, I don't think I could give your sister a good tussle."

"I don't have a sister," I said.

"Wishful thinking," said Cooper with a big grin. "What else do you need from me?"

"Simple. What do you want me to do?"

"I guess the same thing I told the little bald fella. Find out who the guy who looks like a brick is, stop him from bothering me and maybe find out where he got all that information on me."

The sky was now dark, but not from the clouds. Night had come. I glanced at my watch. It said six o'clock but it seldom told me the truth. No amount of fixing had ever done it any good. It had been left to me by my father along with a pile of debts back in '32. I had never learned not to count on the old man, and now it was hard to stop counting on that watch.

"And there's no chance that you'd do the picture for Gelhorn?" I asked, following his directions to his house.

"Nope," he said. "I'm under contract to Goldwyn and I don't want to do the picture. I'm sorry about Lombardi's threat to you, but . . ."

"That's all right," I said, pulling into his driveway. "It's part of the job."

"I'm going to be taking a few days off for some hunting

with a friend in Utah before we start shooting," he said, shaking my hand. "If you have to reach me, call this number." He pulled out a card and handed it to me. "Now about money . . ."

"I don't have a card, at least not one with my real name on it," I said. "How about thirty dollars a day and expenses?"

"The fat fella got forty dollars," Cooper said, working his brittle body out of the Buick.

"Figures," I said. "I'll get the rest of the information I need from him."

Cooper fished a wallet from his finely tailored suit and handed me three twenties.

"I'll give you a detailed accounting when the job ends," I said.

"Good enough," he said and turned to walk to his door. My napkins had not quite done their job. A distinct ameba-shaped grease spot stood out on the rear of Cooper's expensive coat. Lombardi had managed to stain the perfect image by proxy.

I looked at the sixty bucks, examined the autographs of the Yankees and headed into the night. I had to deal with the fake Toby Peters, but that could wait till the morning.

With sixty bucks in my pocket, I went home and called Carmen, the cashier at Levy's Restaurant. Carmen and I had been sparring for nearly three years, and I was determined to move up the pace. After all, Marco from Chicago might be right. The Japanese might land any minute, and even if they didn't, I might be a few dozen kosher-style hot dogs in the near future. The time was now. I invited her to go to the Hitching Post on Hollywood and Vine to see Johnny Mack Brown in *West of Carson City.* She said she wanted to go to the Olympic and see *I Take This Woman* with Spencer Tracy. For some reason Ginger Rogers and George Brent were going to be there in person. We compromised and agreed to go to the Biltmore Bowl to hear Phil Harris and his orchestra and play a little gin rummy.

I was supposed to pick her up at nine. It would have been a fine evening. My assault on the widow Carmen was well planned. I shaved carefully with my Gillette Blue Blade and bathed languidly with my Swan soap. I ignored the pounding of Mr. Hill, the retired accountant, by humming "This Love of Mine" to drown out his passionate plea for the toilet.

I put on my clean suit and headed into the night, managing to avoid Mrs. Plaut. I did not, however, manage to avoid the fist of the man who came up to me as I opened my car door. The first punch to my stomach doubled me over. My face hit the top of the car. The second punch, also delivered to my midsection, had me kissing my knees. I sank to the street. A car passed by. Its headlights spotted my face, but it didn't slow down.

I turned to look at my mugger while gasping to pull in air. There wasn't much I could see from the ground, but his shape was clear. Cooper had been right. He looked like a giant brick.

"You hear me," he said in a high voice that seemed to come from someone else, definitely not from the cement truck that had me doubled over in the street. "Cooper does the picture or I'll turn you into hamburger."

In spite of the pain I managed a laugh, but it must have sounded like a mad gasp. The brick backed away. If Cooper didn't do the picture, Lombardi would turn my hand into hot dogs and my mugger would turn the rest of me into hamburger. I wondered what my cost per pound was on the open market.

"You nuts bastard," he spat, leaning over me, "you keep your nose out or you disappear, you got it?" He gave me a little kick in the kidney to be sure he had my attention. "You got it?"

“Got it,” I said, and he vanished.

I got to my feet and staggered back, almost falling into a passing car. My clothes were dirty and my shirt torn. I managed to find some smog-filled air and enough pride to stand reasonably straight. I made my way back to Mrs. Plaut’s porch and up the stairs, fighting back nausea.

Mrs. Plaut met me in the hall. “Exterminating again?” she said sweetly.

I nodded, unable to speak, as I grasped the railing and started upstairs. I wondered what Mrs. Plaut thought I was exterminating, giant rats in hand-to-hand combat? I was determined to make the date with Carmen, but my body said no, the idiocy you could pull off at twenty-five is off limits at forty-five. This time Mr. Hill wouldn’t let me in the toilet, so I sat in my room hyperventilating for five minutes before I called Carmen and told her I had to work. She said it was okay if I’d promise to take her to the fights Thursday at the Hollywood Legion Stadium. Red Green the “Waterfront Kid” and Mexican George Morelia were the main event. I said sure and hung up.

There are days like this in my business. They come maybe once a year, but they certainly make life interesting. I managed to pry open a 37-cent can of Spam and a dietetically nonfattening bottle of Acme Beer, the beer with the high I.Q. (It Quenches). And then I slept like a baby—a baby cutting new teeth.

CHAPTER THREE

The tenants of the Farraday Building included bookies, alcoholic doctors, baby photographers with astigmatism, con artists who were long on con and short on artistry and third-rate dentists. Actually there was only one dentist in the Farraday at the present time. He had moved down from second-rate to third-rate as a result of filthy fingernails, poor eyesight and an indifference to his victims that would have put the Inquisition to shame. I sublet my office from Sheldon Minck, D.D.S. We were on the fourth floor of the Farraday, which involved a scenic trip up the stairs in order to avoid the decrepit elevator which our landlord, Jeremy Butler, was constantly trying to repair. In fact, Jeremy's principal goal in life was to keep mildew, bums, tenants and time from wearing down the Farraday. Jeremy, former pro wrestler and part-time poet, was barely holding his own.

It was a Tuesday morning, and I felt pretty good, I mean if you discount the sore stomach and kidney; and in my business you either discounted such things or you paid the full price. My three weeks at the Ocean Palms made me welcome the smell of Lysol when I walked up the fake marble stairs.

On the third floor I heard someone singing or moaning deep in the darkness of the corridor near the doorway of Artistic Books, Inc. Artistic Books was run by a gentlewoman named Alice Palice. It was an economical operation, consisting of one small printing press which weighed only 250 pounds. Alice, who looked something like a printing press herself, could easily hoist the press on her shoulder and move it to another office when the going got rough.

Clients almost never came to my office. I discouraged it. When someone called, I usually went to him or arranged a meeting at the drugstore on the corner or Manny's taco stand, depending on how much class the potential client had.

During the three weeks I had been away, Shelly had changed the lettering on our outer door. He was under the delusion that something would catch the eye of passersby and pull them in. Since few drunks could stand the altitude and only bums came up seeking warmth, off-the-street traffic was minimal.

The new lettering read:

Sheldon P. Minck, D.D.S., S.D.
Dentist and Oral Surgeon

and in much smaller letters:

Toby Peters
Private Investigation

Shelly was not an oral surgeon, though he practiced it. I didn't know what the penalty was for impersonating an oral surgeon. Perhaps the dental society took away your mirror on a stick. I knew the "S.D." didn't mean anything and the initial "P" had been a recent idea.

I went through our reception room which we had cleaned up after a few mishaps the year before, but Shelly and I had quickly reduced the small room to its prior state: three wooden chairs, small table with an overflowing ashtray and copies of magazines from previous decades. Past the reception room was Shelly's dental office, and beyond that the closet that served as my office.

Shelly was working on someone in the chair when he heard me close the door. "Be with you in a minute. Have a seat."

I walked over to him and he turned his myopic eyes in my direction, took the wet cigar out of his mouth, wiped his sweating bald head and smiled a sickly grin. "Toby, hey."

"Yeah, Shelly, hey," I said. Then I saw the patient in the chair, an old birdlike guy named Stange who had wrecked the office last year in a pathetic attempt at robbery.

"What's he doing here?" I asked, leaning over Shelly's shoulder.

Stange smiled through his stubbly face, showing his single tooth.

"The challenge was too great, too great," sighed Shelly, seriously pausing to clean the sharp instrument in his hand on his dirty, once-white smock. "This mouth is a challenge I can't refuse. I can build on that tooth, Toby. I know I can. I can construct a mouthful of teeth. I can experiment with new techniques, planting teeth, wires, stuff like that. Mr. Stange and I have an understanding. No more troubles. Right, Karl?"

Karl beamed, and Shelly patted him on the shoulder–a very grubby shoulder.

"I think you should start by putting a wire in his gums, right over there," I said, pointing to a spot in Stange's mouth but being careful not to touch him.

Shelly shrugged and shook his head to show I didn't know what I was talking about. "No anchorage. None. I plan to drill a hole right there." He touched Stange's red-white gums with the sharp instrument, and the old bird jumped four inches.

"Sorry, Shel," I said. "You'll have to put the wire on top."

Shelly turned to me, all five and a half feet filled with indignation.

"Say, who's the dentist around here, you or me?"

"I don't know," I said with a smile. "Who's the detective around here, you or me?"

Shelly turned from me and stuck his head in the Stange-bird beak. "I'm busy," he said.

"Gary Cooper," I said.

"No time for new patients." He waved over his shoulder with his cigar. "I've got all I can handle now." Shelly was nervously jabbing balls of cotton into Stange's mouth. Some of it looked used.

"You're going to choke him," I said, craning my neck to watch Stange's face turn purple. Shelly grunted.

"Shelly," I insisted.

"I gotta work fast," he said. "The First District of the Los Angeles Dental Society is meeting today from four-thirty to ten-thirty at the Hollywood Roosevelt on how dentists can cooperate with doctors in emergencies. Maybe I can pick up some first-aid ideas and expand the business."

I waited for a few seconds while Shelly went after the world's mouth-packing title. Glancing around the office, I saw it hadn't changed. Piles of dental magazines and crossword-puzzle books. Uncleaned instruments in the sink, where the water dripped steadily. Coffee on the hot plate.

"My present plan is to break the coffee pot over your head," I said.

"You've got a message," Shelly responded urgently.

"Maybe I'll break a chair over your head instead. Or maybe I'll break Mister Stange over your head."

Mr. Stange made a flaying effort to rise, but Shelly shoved him back.

"Instrument case in the drawer under the coffee," Shelly mumbled, pointing vaguely.

I shuffled through the pile of napkins, rusty instruments and old campaign literature for Al Smith in the drawer and found the instrument case. Inside it was an envelope marked "TP," and inside the envelope was $267 and three dimes.

"I was holding it for you," Shelly said, his back still to me.

"There should be three hundred or more from Cooper," I said, pocketing the envelope.

"Expenses," he explained. "You know you can't conduct an investigation for nothing. I got a pair of binoculars and . . ."

"Shelly, what the hell did you do it for?"

"Not now, I've got a patient," Shelly stage-whispered.

"Your patient can wait," I said, removing the empty pot on the hot plate. Shelly had drunk all the coffee, and the pot was filling with steam. At least once a year the coffee pot exploded. Once it went out the reception-room window like a cannonball, nearly decapitating Shelly's wife Mildred as she came in.

"Okay, okay," Shelly said with an enormous sigh. He turned and faced me, removing his glasses so he wouldn't have to see how I'd take his explanation. "I wanted to help."

I shook my head no but realized that he couldn't see me, so I said, "No. Try again."

"All right. I wanted to see if I could do it, to meet a movie star. You get to meet movie stars, famous people, and I spend my life in people's mouths and the quality of mouth in this neighborhood could stand upgrading. I mean I love my job, but . . ."

"What about Cary Grant?" I said. "You worked on his mouth, didn't you?"

"That was a lie," Shelly said. I moved across the room, but Shelly continued to talk to the coffee pot, refusing to put his glasses back on.

"So you wanted to meet Gary Cooper and play detective," I said. At the sound of my voice from another part of the room, Shelly put on his glasses and found me. Mr. Stange was gagging behind him.

"I didn't do a bad job," Shelly said.

"Just tell me what you did and what you found out. Tell me fast."

"There's a notebook in your bottom drawer," said Shelly, looking at the stub of his cigar. "I made a report. I think I was getting somewhere, Toby. I really think that a dentist's point of view brings a new perspective to the detective business. I really do."

"Shel, you pull this again and I'll turn dentist and pull all your teeth." I gave him a big smile and went into my office, slamming the door behind me.

Shelly mumbled something about gratitude before he went back to Mr. Strange's foul mouth.

The report was there, in a 1935 ledger book. It was surprisingly good. The words were printed in tiny letters. He had interviewed four people who were interested in getting Cooper to do the film he didn't want to do. The picture was called *High Midnight,* and its producer was Max Gelhorn. Shelly had his address written neatly: an office building on Sunset, the far side of Sunset where you could have the Sunset address but be in a neighborhood few respectable tourists visit. According to Shelly, everyone he talked to cooperated when he put a little pressure on them. Actually there wasn't much information. There was a trade-journal clipping on Gelhorn, indicating that his prime had been reached in the late 1920s, when he had produced a series of two-reel Westerns starring someone named Tall Mickey Fargo.

The next name on Shelly's list was Lola Farmer, an

actress with no major credits, who was to star with Cooper in *High Midnight.* I wondered if this might be the Lola whom Cooper said he had dallied with and who had gone back to Lombardi. Things were already getting complicated. Lola's address was the Big Bear Bar in Burbank. Name number three was none other than Tall Mickey Fargo, who was set to play the villain in *High Midnight.*

A clipping from a shopping-center newsletter which Shelly had plucked had an interview with Fargo that mentioned his forthcoming co-starring role with Cooper. There was a photograph of Fargo in the clipping; and I recognized the thin, dark man with the pencil mustache and the almost-comical oversize cowboy hat. I'd seen him in movies when I was a kid. He had always been one of the gang who got killed in the first shootout with the hero. The last name on the list was Curtis Bowie, who had written the screenplay for *High Midnight.* It was certainly a quartet who needed Cooper for the project. The Los Angeles addresses for both Bowie and Fargo made it clear that they weren't rolling in the wealth of Hollywood.

I copied the addresses, took the clippings and shoved them in my pocket. Then I returned the one call that had come in my three-week absence. It was from a woman named Carol Slingo in San Pedro. Her parrot had been murdered by an intruder, stabbed with a scissors. There was an empty bottle of nassal spray near the cage, indicating that the murderer had first tried to spray the parrot to death. Mrs. Slingo was angry because the police had refused to pursue the matter with "sufficient concern." Her theory was that the parrot had been killed to silence him, to keep him from identifying the intruder. I asked if the parrot could do such a thing and she admitted he couldn't, but the intruder might not know that, especially when he heard the parrot talking. I told her I'd get back to her or have my assistant Mr. Minck look into it as soon as we had time.

While I talked to Mrs. Slingo from San Pedro, I reexamined my office, especially the framed copy of my private investigator's certificate on the wall next to the photograph. I don't keep photographs except for this one. In it my older brother Phil has his arm around me, and I'm holding the collar of our dog Murphy. Murphy was a Beagle I renamed Kaiser Wilhelm when Phil returned wounded from his couple of months in World War I. Our old man is standing next to us, his eyes turned proudly on his sons. Both Phil at fourteen and my old man at fifty were tall and heavy, and I was a scrawny ten-year-old. The main puzzle of the photograph for me is whether my nose had already been broken once by then. I can't tell. I've asked people, even my brother, who was the first to break the nose. Phil doesn't care or remember. He has broken too many noses since then to recall the date of such a minor event.

I left the office with a glance at Shelly's back. He was hunched over Mr. Stange, cooing, "Just a little wider, a little wider, uh, hu, just a. . . ."

The groaner was gone from the third floor, and the Farraday was coming to something resembling life. Life at the Farraday began sluggishly a little before noon and never got into high gear. In the lobby I encountered Jeremy Butler, massive hands on massive hips, looking critically at the dark tile floor.

"Toby," he said, "you think it needs a scrubbing today? I did it yesterday, but . . ."

"It looks fine, Jeremy, fine. How's the poetry business?"

"It's not a business. It's an act of expression. *North States Review* is publishing my poem on the war. It's a damn war, Toby."

"That it is," I agreed.

"U-boats near the Panama Canal," he sighed, kneeling to examine a scuff mark. "You know they're considering martial law in southern California to control enemy aliens and American-born Japanese? The *Times* says there are 100,-000. You think they'll put Hal Yamashura in jail? They might if this gets crazy enough."

"I don't know, Jeremy," I said.

Jeremy raised his huge, well-balanced bulk and turned toward me. "Man was looking for you yesterday. A guy with violence steaming in him. I could feel it."

"Solid guy, looked like a big brick?" I tried.

"That's him," he said. "You need some help?"

"I don't think so. If I do, I know where to find you."

I went out into the cold, buttoned my coat, pulled down my hat and went for my Buick. I had a pocketful of dollars, a case to work on and a dead parrot for backup. That was enough to keep my mind off the war for a few hours.

My first stop was Max Gelhorn's office on Sunset. It was a thin, undernourished office building huddled between a one-story short-order diner with a 25-cent breakfast special and a bar with brown windows that advertised Eastside Beer and Ale.

Gelhorn's office was an elevator ride to the third floor and a walk down an uncarpeted corridor. A chunky girl with a cold sat behind the reception desk. She wore a blue suit. Behind her I could see Gelhorn's open office. The operation was as small as it could be. Gelhorn Productions was not in the bucks.

"I'm here to see Max Gelhorn," I said, looking around with as much superiority as I could master.

"He is on location," she sniffled.

"Location?"

"He is shooting a Western movie," she explained. "For PRC."

"And where might this location be?" I asked.

She groped for a fresh Kleenex just in time to keep from offending me. "Not at liberty to say," she said.

"My name is Fligdish, from the Fourth Commercial Bank of New York City," I said sweetly. "If Mr. Gelhorn wants to talk about refinancing *High Midnight,* it will be today or not at all. I have other appointments and a plane to catch this evening." I looked at my father's watch with impatience. It told me it was half past five. I moved it slightly and I saw that the no-longer-attached hour hand spun around when I jiggled it.

"Burbank," she said, scribbling a street-corner address on a pad and tearing the paper off to hand to me.

"Thank you," I said. "Take care of that cold."

"How?" she said miserably as I left the office.

The odds were pretty good that one of the four people Shelly had interviewed was behind the man-who-looked-like-a-brick. They were the people who knew he/I/someone was on the case. I had nothing else to go on, anyway. My engine was making a slight pinging sound that had in the past gradually become a forty-three-dollar symphony. Maybe I could finish this case before putting the car in dry dock.

I turned on the radio long enough to find that Dolph Camilli, the National League's Most Valuable Player with 34 home runs and 120 runs batted in, had signed again with the Brooklyn Dodgers for $20,000. I was too old to become a baseball player and too homely to be a movie star.

The street corner in Burbank was behind a factory. The street corner was actually a huge vacant lot leading up to a hill with a few trees on it. The hill went up sharply to about the height of a three-story building. Plunked in the middle of this vacant lot were four horses, a half-dozen guys with cowboy outfits, a man with a camera and an assortment of other people shivering in a small circle next to a wooden shack, which was being moved around by a thin girl and two guys in sweaters.

When I parked and moved toward them, one man separated himself from the pack and strode toward me with a smile. Behind his back he whispered, "Set it up fast, Herman." The wind had been blowing my way or I wouldn't have heard him. He was a little taller, a little younger and seemed to be a lot more enthusiastic than I was about life, but then again he was clearly faking.

"I," he said, holding out a hand, "am Max Gelhorn. Can I be of some service to you?"

Behind him the sweatered crew tied horses to a quickly constructed rail in front of the shack, cowboys checked their guns and the camera was lugged back to take it all in.

"You have a permit to shoot here?" I asked sternly.

"Permit?" Gelhorn looked puzzled. He was wearing a coat over his heavy woolen sweater. His yellow-gray hair was massive and blowing wild. "I checked with Mr. Payson and he said–"

"Payson?" I said suspiciously. "There is no Mr. Payson."

"Maybe I got the name wrong," Gelhorn mused, glancing over his shoulder to see how quickly things were being set up.

"You don't have permission to shoot here, do you?" I said through clenched teeth.

"Well, not exactly," said Gelhorn, "but we'll be out of here in an hour at the most and . . . . Say, how would you like to be in this picture? You'd be perfect. Not much, just a small part in this shot holding a horse. Doris," he shouted, and the girl in the sweater came running. She was a pale, panting, pinched creature with rimless glasses and pigtails. Her age was something between eighteen and thirty. "Doris," Gelhorn repeated with mock enthusiasm, "I think this gentleman would be perfect as the bandit holding the horses. What do you think?"

"Perfect," agreed Doris, picking up her cue.

"Well, Mr. . . ." Gelhorn began.

"Peters," I said. The name killed a birdie in his head but he chalked it up to minor coincidence. I forced the issue. "Toby Peters," I said.

"Who are you?" Gelhorn demanded, dropping the hand-wringing act and taking on steam without heat.

"Toby Peters, private investigator."

"You've changed in a week," sneered Gelhorn. "You used to be short, fat, obnoxious and stupid. You are no longer fat."

"That was my junior partner, using my name while I was on vacation," I explained. "I'd be careful how you talk about him in his presence. He's a jujitsu expert."

"Really," said Gelhorn. "Well, it has been unpleasant talking to you, but I've got to get back to my film." He turned, and Doris followed, looking back at me with curiosity.

"I had a talk with Mr. Lombardi yesterday," I said. That stopped Gelhorn so dead in his tracks that he almost toppled over. He turned to me with a quizzical look. "Lombardi? I don't know any—"

"Of course not," I said. "You want to talk before I report back to Mr. Cooper that I found you most uncooperative? You don't want to kill your chances of getting Cooper for *High Midnight.*"

Gelhorn hurried back to me and panted, "Then he *is* considering the offer?"

I shrugged. "Depends on what I tell him."

"I made a straight offer," said Gelhorn as blandly as he could.

"What made you think the highest-salaried actor in Hollywood, the actor who is probably going to win his second Academy Award, is going to make a low-budget Western with you? What's in it for him?"

"That," said Gelhorn, "is between Mr. Cooper and me."

"It can't be that you got the idea of putting pressure on Cooper to come into this?"

From a hot-dog stand on the corner, the sound of music cut through the wind.

"I don't need Gary Cooper," Max Gelhorn said, plunging his hands into his pockets.

"Of course not," I agreed. "I can see that. I've seen that plush office of yours, and I can see the epic you're shooting in an empty lot."

A whistle blew behind us and drowned out his answer. Seconds later workers from the factory were streaming out and heading for the hot-dog stand for lunch. Some of them glanced at the movie crew and hurried to get their sandwiches so they could spend their break watching.

"Perhaps we could talk after I get this scene," Gelhorn said, looking anxiously at the workers and probably fearing that a factory foreman would appear to boot him off the vacant lot.

"Okay," I said.

"We'll have a cup of coffee," he said amiably, backing away. "Uh, and how about holding the horse in this shot. We're a bit short-handed, and you look perfect."

"Why not," I said with a grin that never looked like a grin.

Doris fished out a cowboy hat and vest and took my coat and jacket. Gelhorn told me to stand on the far side of the horses so my pants and shoes wouldn't show on camera. Then Gelhorn went mad with activity. The cameraman, a little guy with a heavy German accent, began arguing with him about how little space there was to shoot.

"You want the cowboys should ride behind a hot-dog stand?" he squeaked. "Or up the hill to that garage?"

"I know it's tight, Hugo, but that's what we've got. Just do it. I'll buy you a cup of coffee after."

An overweight actor in a cowboy suit lumbered up to Gelhorn, waving a script. "Max," he cried, "how the hell am I supposed to do this? You said you'd get a stunt man. I can't—"

"Mickey," whispered Gelhorn, "a stunt man is at least

twenty bucks, even a lousy stuntman. You've done harder than this before. I'll give you an extra te . . . five."

I adjusted my cowboy hat and stepped out from behind the horses to get a better look at Tall Mickey Fargo. It was the same man whose picture I had in my pocket, but someone had put a balloon inside him and blown it up. He was a bloated caricature. I couldn't imagine him getting on a horse, let alone doing a stunt, but the five dollars proved too much for him, and he agreed.

It was cold without my coat, so I huddled back among the horses. One of them tried to nuzzle me. I've got nothing against animals as long as they leave me alone. I think human responsibilities are too much and I never understood why anyone would choose to take on responsibility for an animal. Unfortunately, all animals love me. Maybe I just smell from salty sweat. A factory worker with a bottle of Nehi and a sandwich came up to me and asked what we were shooting.

"A Hoot Gibson movie," I said. "Hoot's not in this shot."

Gelhorn had backed off with Hugo and the camera and waved wildly for the factory worker to get out of the shot. The factory worker, a stocky guy with black curly hair, raised his fist at Gelhorn and laughed before backing away.

"No sound in this shot," shouted Gelhorn over the music from the hot-dog stand and the laughs and conversation of factory workers. "Remember, Mickey, you've set a dynamite charge in the shack, and you want to get away fast. You come out of the door, go for your horse, get shot and tumble down. Then you look back at the shack in fear. You know it is going to blow any second and you're not sure you can get away. You with the horses," Gelhorn shouted, seemingly forgetting who I was in the heat of shooting, "get in the shot." I moved forward.

"Okay," shouted Gelhorn, his voice cracking. "We have

to shoot this tight, Mickey, one take, not much room up and down. Do it right the first time."

Mickey nodded, went over to check his horse and waddled to the shack.

"Camera ready," shouted Gelhorn.

"Ready," grunted Hugo.

"Camera rolling," shouted Gelhorn.

"Rolling," said Hugo.

"Action," said Gelhorn. "Doris, action, get the damn sticks in there."

Doris ran out in front of the camera with the clapboards.

"You don't have to clap them," Gelhorn screamed. "We're not rolling sound. Just get out of there." Doris looked hurt as she scrambled behind the camera with the crew and other extras.

"All right, Mickey, for God's sake," screamed Gelhorn, "get your ass out there! We're wasting film."

Fargo came scurrying out of the cabin, looked back at it with fear worthy of Emil Jannings and went for his horse. It took him two tries to make it onto the horse. Then Gelhorn shouted, "Now, Mickey, now. You've been shot." And the sound of a gunshot cut through the music and noise. Mickey went down off the horse with a grunt and the horse next to me also went down, almost toppling over on me. I jumped out of the way and saw the spot of blood on the horse's shoulder. Then a second shot came and dug dirt a foot away from me. The shots were coming from the top of the hill. No one else seemed to notice them, but then everyone was watching Mickey Fargo try to lift his fallen girth for a look at the shack.

I thought I saw the glint of something metal on the hilltop. My choices weren't many. I could stand still and watch the guy with the gun pick off me and the remaining horses. I could run across the open field and hope to survive, or I could do the stupid thing I did. Maybe it was the costume or the scene or the audience. I got on the nearest horse, remembering vaguely that you mount on the left, and urged the animal forward by whacking its rump. It laughed at me, or made a sound like laughter, and took off running right in front of the camera.

Gelhorn screamed, "Cut, cut, cut, cut, cut."

I tugged the reins to the left toward the hill, and the horse, much to my surprise, turned left. The crowd of factory workers cheered. In about thirty yards I pulled back on the reins and the horse came to an abrupt stop. My arms grabbed the saddle, and I eased myself down as quickly as I could, tossing the cowboy hat away as I scrambled for the cover of bushes and trees. Another shot hit behind me. I went up the hill slowly without looking back, but I could hear Gelhorn's crazed voice behind me coming closer, shouting "Madman."

No more shots came as I worked my way up slowly. From behind a tree I estimated where the rifleman had been and worked behind the spot. A car started not far away, and I jumped from behind the tree to see a Ford coupe pull away with a screech. I barely caught the square shape in the driver's seat. With less caution I went to the spot from where the gun had been fired.

Gelhorn had scrambled up the hill behind me and was advancing, ready to beat me with the clapboard he had probably ripped from the hand of timid Doris.

"You crazy son of a bitch," he screamed. "You know what you cost me? You ruined the shot."

"At least the one someone took at me," I said, kneeling down to pick up some still warm, spent cartridges. I held one up for him to see.

"Bull," he said, moving clapboard-armed on me.

"Go tell the horse that got shot," I said.

Gelhorn stopped. "Horse, shot?" He groaned. "Is it dead?"

"I don't think so. It looked as if the shot barely caught him on the shoulder." I put the shells in my pocket.

"Do you know what I had to do to get those horses?" Gelhorn wailed. "I can't afford to pay for a goddamn horse. It's either horses or cars no matter what you do."

"I appreciate your sympathy," I said, moving back toward the slope of the hill.

"Sympathy?" asked Gelhorn.

"Someone tried to kill me, not ruin your shot," I reminded him.

"Oh, yes," he said, tucking the clapboard under his arm. "I'm sorry about. . . . Maybe we can put a piece of tape over the horse's wound and paint over it. What color is the horse?"

"Black, I think."

"We have black paint," Gelhorn mused to himself.

I outdistanced Gelhorn down the hill and made directly for Mickey Fargo. Tall Mickey, who was now Fat Mickey, had managed with some help to get off the ground.

"Maybe we can match it," he was telling Doris. "Then I won't have to take that fall again. Goddamn horse."

"Mr. Fargo," I said, looking back over my shoulder to see how far Gelhorn was behind me. "Sorry about that. Max will explain when he gets here. I'm a great fan of yours. and I'd like to talk to you at your place later about the Gary Cooper movie."

He turned his chunky bulldog face to me suspiciously. "I don't have . . ." he began.

"I work for Mr. Cooper," I said quickly.

His rheumy eyes opened as wide as his heavy lids would allow, and a grin appeared, revealing remarkably perfect teeth, almost certainly false. "Right," he said. "Catch me later."

I was at my car before Gelhorn could reach me, but I didn't have to hurry. He had zipped past Fargo and his crew and was in a dead run for the fallen horse. He was already calling for a bandage and water colors.

Since I was close, I headed for the Big Bear Bar in Burbank. Maybe I could convince Lola Farmer to change her name to Barbara Banks, then I could say I had seen Barbara Banks at the Big Bear Bar in Burbank. Maybe I could pass the joke on to my nephews. But maybe at twelve and ten, Nate and Dave were already too old for it.

The squat man who was trying to pressure Cooper into making *High Midnight* was obviously not fooling around. Not even Sergeant York could shoot from that range and purposely miss me by a foot. No, no, my friends, this was a fresh message from Lombardi or a new player that I should keep what remained of my nose outside of the business of Gary Cooper. I should have been scared, and I was, but just a little. Another part of me was happy as a dung beetle with a fresh find. This was it. This was the tingling feeling that made me drunk and powerful. I had to ride it while I felt it or fear would take over, but right now I was immortal.

I had a wife once. It was seeing me in moments like this that sent her looking for saner pastures. There were other reasons, but this was a big one. Toby Peters, king of the hill, was ready.

I stopped at a drive-in on Buena Vista and munched a burger with fries and a Pepsi.

"Peters," came a voice near my ear.

Costello was leaning into my window on the left. On the right I could see Marco's belly. His head and shoulders were above the car.

"I thought Mr. Lombardi told you that Cooper is making that movie," Costello said. "That's what he told him, isn't it, Marco?"

"Assuredly," came Marco's voice from above.

"Assuredly," I agreed with a mouthful of hamburger. "I'm just making that clear to the people involved. You want some fries?"

Costello took some fries.

"Marco had a hell of a time keeping up with you," Costello said, still leaning over.

"I'll go slower," I said. "But someone is trying to kill me, and I won't want to stay anywhere for too long."

Costello's eyes narrowed. "You saying we're trying to knock you off?" He pointed to Marco's stomach and to his own chest.

"No," I said, trying not to drip ketchup on my coat. "Some guy who looks like a two-by-four and very much wants Cooper to make that movie."

"Mr. Lombardi won't like that," said Costello, reaching for more of my fries. "He wants you alive to work on Cooper."

"Help yourself," I said, holding out the fries.

"You point out this guy and we'll see to it he stays out of your way. Right, Marco?"

"We'll absent him from the scene," Marco said.

"He shouldn't be too hard to find," I said, cleaning my hands on a napkin and gurgling down the last of the Pepsi. "He'll be the guy behind me with the rifle. Hey, you mind throwing this stuff away so I don't have to get out of the car?"

Costello took the remains of my lunch. I turned on the ignition and backed away, leaving him holding the bag. I decided to drive slowly to the Big Bear Bar so the gentlemen from Chicago could protect my tail. In an odd way it seemed as if we were on the same side. It didn't reassure me much, but it didn't cost anything, either.

CHAPTER FOUR

There weren't any boys whooping it up at the old Big Bear Saloon when I got there a little after one. I turned off Fourth and parked on Noyes in front of a building that shouldn't have been there. The street was full of residential, one-story homes with front lawns big enough for one medium-sized human to stretch out for a sunbath. But it was too cold for sunbathing.

The Big Bear had either predated or fought the residential zoning. It was a two-story dark brick building with a drawing of a big bear in gold on the picture window. Venetian blinds, probably permanently closed, kept the passersby from looking inside. There were no beer signs on the outside to give away the identity of the place; nothing but a Ballantine Ale thermometer next to the entrance.

I tried the door. It opened, and I was into darkness and the sound of a slightly off piano. I stood for a while listening and waiting for my eyes to adjust. Then the piano was joined by the equally off voice of a woman singing "White Cliffs of Dover." She sang on with determination, challenging the tune, getting it down for a while and then having it slip from her control. By the time she got to the end, I was ready to call it a victory for her and a loss for the song. By that time, too, I could see something of the room. It was small, with six tables and a bar running the width of the place. At the end of the room was a grand piano which took up space that could have been used for another couple of tables. At the piano was a woman, or the shadow of a woman whose head was thrown back.

"What do you think?" she asked, in a throaty voice that might have been a good imitation of Betty Field or Jean Arthur or a bad one of Tallulah Bankhead.

"I liked it," I lied, sitting at a red leather stool at the bar.

"Bartender won't be here for a few hours," she said. I still couldn't see her face, but the slowness of her words suggested that she had started her day's sustenance before the barkeep's arrival.

"No hurry," I said, taking off my hat and putting it on the bar.

"You selling something?" she said.

"Nope," I said. "Just looking."

"For what?"

"You, if you're Lola Farmer," said I.

"I'm Lola Farmer," she said suspiciously, stepping down the bar with a hand on each stool as she moved. She meant it to look elegant. It looked like someone with a few too many trying to keep from falling over. In ten steps she was close enough to see me and to be seen.

Lola Farmer was a blonde. Cooper had told me that, but Lola Farmer, like Tall Mickey Fargo, had gone through some changes. Lola had weathered them better. At least that was my guess. She was no longer thin, but she wasn't fat either. Lola was a few thousand calories on the good side of pleasingly plump. Her face was pale and there was darkness beneath her eyes that wouldn't go away with sunlight, but she was a good-looking woman. She had probably started with a lot, and though she looked like she was working to wear it away, she had too much going for her from nature to make the job easy.

"You look like a mug," she said.

"I am a mug," I agreed.

"Did he send you?" she asked.

"Yeah," I said, looking into her eyes, which I guessed were blue.

"What does he want now?" she said, sinking onto the bar stool next to me.

"The same as before," I answered.

"Tell him the answer's the same," she said with a great sigh.

"Suit yourself," I said, playing with my hat.

We sat in silence for a few minutes while I tried to figure out what we had said and what to say next.

"He tell you I sing here?" she said.

"Yeah."

She got up and moved back to the piano to collect the drink she had left there. "What's your name?" she asked, after taking a healthy belt.

"Peters," I said. "Toby Peters."

My eyes were pretty used to the lack of light now and I could see that the name was familiar. She was also confused. Now some confused people retreat. Others break down. Lola attacked.

"Who the hell are you? What do you want? He didn't send you. Get the hell out of here." She took a few angry steps in my direction and threatened me with a near-empty tumbler.

"Who did you think sent me, Lombardi?"

She took the next four steps in front of me without falling and took a swing with the tumbler, missing by a good foot. I slid off the stool and grabbed her before she went down. She smelled of bourbon and perfume, and she felt properly soft. My face was in her hair and I helped her up slowly.

"Thanks," she said, forgetting her anger for a second. I held her hand to steady her. There was a lot left to Lola of whatever it was that had attracted Cooper and Lombardi. "Now get out."

"A few questions first," I said, letting go of her hand. "I'm not looking for trouble."

She shrugged and went around the bar looking for a fresh tumbler. "You want a drink?" she offered.

"A Pepsi if you have one," I grinned.

"You a boxer?" she said, looking at me with a little interest.

"No," I said, "but I've been a punching bag."

"Me too," she said, handing me a bottle of Pepsi with a puffing out of her cheeks. "Cheers."

"You got a bottle opener back there or should I bite off the top with my teeth?"

She took the bottle back and opened it. I accepted and took a drink. The Pepsi was warm.

"You talk first," she said.

"My name is Toby Peters. The man who talked to you was my assistant, who took on a little too much when I was away on a big assignment. I'm on the case now, and I need some answers."

She shrugged, so I went on after another gulp of warm Pepsi.

"Someone is putting pressure on Gary Cooper to be in *High Midnight,* using threats and blackmail involving you. Someone hired an unpleasant character with fists like steam radiators to see to it that Cooper takes the *High Midnight* job. My assistant talked to four people about the project. All four want the film made with Cooper. After he talked to them, the unpleasant character I mentioned showed up and told me to mind my own business. He even tried to put a bullet or two through me less than an hour ago to make his meaning clear."

"You know, Daisy Mae is missing," Lola said, chewing at her upper lip and examining her drink. "You're a detective. Maybe you can help Li'l Abner find her."

"Put it back in the bottle, Lola," I said softly. "You're not that shellacked."

The anger started to come to her eyes again, but she controlled it and looked at me.

"There's you," I said. "There's Max Gelhorn, Tall Mickey Fargo and Curtis Bowie, the writer. You want Cooper in on this project. How badly?"

Lola laughed, a nice deep laugh. "Badly," she said, losing about fifty percent of her drunkenness. "Max is in debt to whoever he got to back the film. He promised to deliver Cooper, and if he can't deliver on the promise, he has big trouble. The man with the money will be very angry. Max got me in on this for two reasons. *A,* I gave him my few dollars in savings, and *B,* he had heard that I knew Cooper. I went to Cooper and offered myself and a memory of old times, but he said no. He turned me down. Lola has lost it."

"Not quite," I said.

"Thanks," she said. "You're pretty cute too in a grotesque sort of way."

"And . . ."

"And," she continued after taking another drink, "Gelhorn is in trouble, and I am out my money and a last chance to make it in the movies. Tall Mickey is a loser who goes way back with Gelhorn. He had no money to lose. He's living on dreams and the hope of a comeback, but–between us–Tall Mickey had nothing to come back to or from. He was never more than a face in the barroom crowd."

"Bowie?" I said, draining my Pepsi and examining the bubbles on the bottom.

"Kicking around for years," she said. "Wrote a few

dime Westerns. Did a Wheeler and Woolsey script. *High Midnight* is his big project. Been working years at it. It's not bad, but what the hell do I know. I think Bowie is screwy enough to kill to get the picture made with Cooper. I guess we're all screwy enough. That what you wanted?"

The last question had a touch of something in it. Maybe it was an invitation. It might even have been sarcasm. I have discovered through the many hard years that I am a rotten judge of the motives of women.

"Did you hire the muscle?" I asked.

She shook her head no and said, almost to herself, "I used my ammunition on Cooper. I haven't got much, but I've got some pride. It's barely holding me together."

"It's doing better than that," I said honestly. She smiled with a nice set of teeth and reached over the bar to touch my cheek. The other hand held tightly to her amber tumbler.

"That's sweet," she said.

"Lombardi," I said, and her hand moved away slowly. "Why does he want you to make the picture?"

"My suggestion to you is to stay away from Mr. Lombardi if you want to hold onto what remains of your appeal," she said. "He can be an unkind man."

I stood up. "He's not giving me a choice."

"Mr. Lombardi thinks he owes me something, and he wants to be a West Coast big shot," she explained. "He wants to make movies and sell cheese."

"Hot dogs," I corrected. "He has a hot-dog factory."

She laughed. "His old man had a hot-dog stand on Coney Island," she said.

"Funny," I said. "Thanks. I'll see you around."

Before I hit the door, her voice caught me.

"I'm through here at eleven," she said. "If you want to come back, I'll buy you a Pepsi."

"Eleven," I said, without looking back, and I went out into the light. If it had been a sunny day, I would have been as helpless as a Universal Studio vampire. As it was, I had to stand still for a few seconds. The piano tinkled an off-beat version of *Blues in the Night,* and I hurried away before Lola started to sing.

I drove through the hills and out of the valley with the down-and-out image of Lola Farmer. I wasn't sure what there was about her that got to me. It was something distant and sad, something I wanted to find and examine. I didn't quite feel sorry for her, but there was something about her that was comforting, like sinking into a hot bath and losing yourself.

The area of Los Angeles I drove to brought me back to reality. Clapboard houses and dark brick churches looked pretty good on a clear day, but a day like this showed the neighborhood for what it was, a ghetto of out-of-work losers even at a time when jobs were easy to get and men were scarce. The kids in the street and little parks wore someone else's coat. Weary wives with handkerchiefs on their heads carried packages and clinging kids.

Curtis Bowie's house was easy to find. It was just off Sixty-fifth, a very small wooden house painted white but showing rotting wood underneath. There was no room for the house to breathe. It was almost flush with twin houses on both sides.

I parked, locked the Buick and went up to the screen door. My knock rattled the screen, which looked ready to fall out and had so many holes it couldn't have discouraged an eagle, let alone a fly.

"Anyone home?" I asked, peering through the screen and seeing a living room of gray furniture. I knocked again and opened the door. One of the hinges was completely off. I caught the door in time and carefully replaced it behind me as I walked in. The living room was small and decorated in fake Victorian decay. The sofa had a spot so worn the round outline of the springs was clear. A newspaper was on the floor, as if someone had been reading it when he was called away by the phone, bodily needs or food boiling over.

"Mister Bowie?" I called. "Are you here?"

No answer. I walked through the living room and found myself in the kitchen, where a man was seated at a small wooden table, his head down and his hands at his side.

"Mister Bowie?" I said, and the body stirred.

"Who?" said Bowie, lifting his head to look at his dish-filled sink instead of at me.

"I'm over here," I said, and his eyes turned in the right direction and tried to focus on me. He was a lean man, a leathery lean man with a slightly silly smile and a head of curly gray hair. He wore a pair of work pants, a flannel shirt and suspenders. His sleeves were rolled up as if he were about to work on something electrical or mechanical. Beneath him on the table I could see sheets of notebook paper with scribbles and crossed-out words.

"Tomorrow for sure," he said, standing with a yawn. "I'm picking up a check this morning and I'll pay you tomorrow after I cash it at the bank."

"It's afternoon now, Mr. Bowie," I said.

He was waking up now and looked over at me to be sure which debtor I was. He didn't recognize me. To help his memory he walked to the sink, pushed over a pile of fly-attracting dishes and turned on the cold water. He cupped his hands, filled them with water, plunged his face into his palms and said, "Buggggle, pllubie."

He stood up and stretched.

"Now," he said amiably in an accent that touched of the Southwest, "how can I help you?"

"My name is Toby Peters," I said, holding out my hand to shake.

He took it and said, "No it's not."

"Yes it is," I insisted with a false little laugh. "The fellow who told you he was me was a dentist who wanted to play detective while I was busy on another case."

"You mind if I use that?" he said, reaching for his pencil on the table and pulling a sheet of paper in front of him. "A dentist pretending to be a detective. I thought there was something funny about him. Now that I think of it he did say something about my jaw protruding, said I should see an oral surgeon."

"Can I ask you a few questions, Bowie?"

"Sure," said Bowie, "have a seat. Like some coffee?"

I tried not to look around at the sink and the fly convention on the nearby cabinets as I declined.

"I do not get a lot of visitors," Bowie explained as we both sat. "A writer often leads a solitary life."

"High Midnight," I said, taking off my hat and unbuttoning my coat.

"High Midnight," Bowie sighed, playing with his suspenders. "Best thing I've ever done. Took me three, four years on and off. Wrote it with Gary Cooper in mind. Little fat fella who said he was you told me he was working for Cooper."

"Right," I said. "I'm working for Cooper, trying to find out who's putting some ugly pressure on him to make *High Midnight."*

"I'd like him to make it," said Bowie through his smile. "That's a fact. Max Gelhorn told me he had Cooper all lined up. I've got no advance on this project, Peters, not a wooden dime. I'm just sitting here and waiting."

"Any idea who might be willing to buy some muscle and dirt to put pressure on Cooper?" I asked, watching Bowie snap his suspenders.

"I might," said Bowie, "but I couldn't buy the services of a blind pickpocket. I am down to my last two bucks."

"That could make a man desperate," I said, looking into his eyes.

"It can make a man hungry," replied Bowie. "You think there's any chance of Cooper making the movie?"

I got up and said I didn't know. Bowie got up too.

"I do have coffee," he said. "I mean if you had said you wanted a cup. I even have sugar."

"I never doubted it," I said, returning his grin. "What do you think of Lola Farmer and Mickey Fargo?"

"Never met them," said Bowie, running his hand through his hair. "I know they're supposed to be in the picture, but nothing's gone far enough for us to meet."

"You have a copy of *High Midnight* around I could read?" I asked, making a step toward the living room.

"Sure," he said, moving ahead of me into the room. "Read it and tell me what you think. Maybe you can put in a good word for it with Mr. Cooper if you like it."

Bowie ambled to a bookcase in the corner and found the script at the top of a pile of what looked like typed scripts.

"I've only got two left," he explained, handing it to me and nearly getting his feet tangled in the newspaper on the floor.

"Hey," I said, pulling out my wallet. "I'm not asking for a free copy."

"No," he said, rubbing his hands on the back of his pants.

"I'm on an expense account," I explained. "Will five bucks cover it?"

"Cover it fine," Bowie said.

He ushered me to the door and gently opened it so it wouldn't fall.

"I've been meaning to fix that," he said.

We shook hands, and I went into the street with a wave back at Bowie, who returned the wave. I hoped he didn't turn out to be the one I was looking for.

There was no traffic on the small street, so I had no trouble spotting Marco and Costello in the Packard behind me. I drove back to my old neighborhood in Hollywood, where Costello and Marco waited outside while I went into Ralph's and bought two pounds of Washington Delicious apples for 14 cents. There was a phone at the exit of the grocery, and I had a dime in my change. I put down my small package, found a number in my phone book and called Ann Peters, to whom I had been married for five painful years.

"TWA, Miss Peters, can I help you?"

"Mitzenmacher," I corrected. "Your name is Mitzenmacher. I got my name back when we were divorced."

"Toby, are you drunk?"

"No, and you can keep on using my name. It's the only worthwhile thing I gave you."

"Toby," she said, whispering so someone on her end couldn't hear. "I'm busy." I imagined her long dark hair and full figure in a well-tailored suit.

"I'm at Ralph's buying groceries, and I thought about your boyfriend Ralph, and then I thought about you," I said.

"Very romantic," she said. "I'm hanging up and going home. Don't call again."

"Wait," I shouted and a lady going past me gave me a dirty look. "I'm sorry. How about dinner tonight? Ozzie Nelson's at the Florentine Gardens."

"I thought you weren't going to bother me anymore."

"I don't know where you got that idea," I said. "Tonight, just to talk over good times?"

"There were no good times," she whispered. "Now I'm hanging up."

"I'll just call back. I've got a lot of dimes."

"Toby, please . . ."

"If you don't see me, you'll drive me into the arms of a boozy singer."

"I'm going to marry Ralph," she said. "In March."

I said nothing.

"Toby? Are you still there?"

"Yeah," I said.

"I'm going to hang up. Don't call back."

"I won't," I said, and she hung up while I gagged on something gracious to say.

I went out into the parking lot and took my package to Costello and Marco's car. "You guys want an apple?"

Marco took one. Costello declined.

"Women," I said, taking an apple for myself. "Never marry them."

"My old man never took nuptials," said Marco sympathetically.

"I'm going home for dinner," I said. "If you guys want to take a break, I'll be there for a few hours at least, maybe for the night."

I was feeling sorry for myself and conjuring disaster and death for Ann's Ralph. I had seen Ralph once in the hall of her apartment in Culver City. He was everything I wasn't: prosperous, tall, handsome, a great head of distinguished gray hair, tan. Maybe a TWA plane would run over him before March. He was too old to be drafted.

The hell with it. I told the car not to do it, but it was possessed. I gave it its own head like Tony in a Tom Mix picture from when I was a kid. My faithful Buick took me to Culver City.

The game had turned more serious with each assault on the stronghold of Ann Mitzenmacher Peters. Weeping, lies, tears, pain, reminders of the bad old days and rolls in the bed which she had rudely forgotten or pretended to forget, had all failed. Threats had made her laugh. The worst part about it, I thought as I went into the small, clean lobby of the long, recently built white building was that Ann seemed to be beyond the point of even getting angry with me. What is the worth of a man when he can't even draw blood or anger, let alone passion or sympathy?

I rang the bell and dashed up to the second floor when she responded with a ring. Ann stood in the hall, one hand on a hip, her hair long and dark, her figure full at forty. In the last few years I had seen her nowhere but in this hall or apartment, and I didn't much care for the apartment.

"I can't stay. I'm going," I said before she could speak. I hurried up to her, looking at my watch.

"That watch doesn't work, Toby," she said, "and generally, neither do you. Out."

"What have I done to deserve insults?" I said. "Goodbye." I kissed her on the cheek and stood back. "I was in the neighborhood and wanted to show I had no hard feelings, that I really wish you and Rollo well."

"Ralph," she corrected emotionlessly.

"Ralph," I said. "I'd like to come to the wedding. I would . . ."

Her head nodding no. She had no right to stand there in a yellow suit looking as good as she looked.

"I have about ten minutes," I said. "Want to invite me in?"

Her head said no, and she folded her arms patiently.

"I'm working for Gary Cooper," I said with a shake of my head. "He . . ."

She shook her head no again.

"Was I really such a bad guy, Ann?" I said.

"No," she said. "And you don't give up easily. That was one of the things I liked about you, at least for a while. Now it's starting to be one of the things I like least. Toby, I don't hate you. You went out of my life five years ago."

"Four years," I corrected.

"I don't care if it's only ten minutes," she said. "It seems like five years. Just turn around and go away. Don't cry, lie or ask for a drink of water. Don't threaten, beg or tell me about the afternoon we fell in the pond in MacArthur Park. Just go."

"Isn't your life just a little boring?" I said, stepping toward her and glancing into her room enough to see that it was still decorated in unwelcoming browns and whites.

"No," she said. "It is peaceful, and you are not part of it."

"Are you going to stop calling yourself Peters when you marry Waldo?"

"Toby, you know damn well his name is Ralph," she said wearily. "Now leave. I'll stop calling myself Peters when I marry Ralph."

"What's Ralph's last name?" I asked, clinging to the conversation.

"No, you might just decide to make a pest of yourself."

"I wouldn't do that, Ann. I just want to know. Besides, I'm a detective. I can find Ralph's last name without any trouble. I won't feel right if you wind up with some name like Reed or Brown. Ann Brown sounds like a character in Brenda Starr, for God's sake."

She didn't even bother to answer. Instead she looked at her watch, which was working. Then she looked at me as if to say, "Is there anything more to this act?"

I shrugged, defeated again.

"I'm going in now," she said, reaching out to touch my shoulder. "Don't knock. Don't ring and please don't return. Just go play with your guns and dentists and midgets. Go play cops and robbers, and once and for all get out of my life."

There was a touch of hope in her blast—at least it was a blast with emotion. But the door slammed in my face, and I was standing there alone.

"Don't knock," she said through the door as I raised my hand. "I'm going to turn on the water and take a long bath. Don't be here when I get out or I'll call the police again."

CHAPTER FIVE

Mrs. Plaut wasn't home. If she had been, I probably would have strangled her. I was in no mood for tolerance. I decided to offer Gunther an apple, but he was out. So I sat in my room for about fifteen minutes, still wondering what Ralph's last name was. Smiler? Johnson? Stoneworthy? Ann probably picked him for his name. This was getting me nowhere, and I had gone through four apples. I grabbed Curtis Bowie's manuscript of *High Midnight* and took a long bath.

Since it took a millennium for the bathtub to dribble to half-capacity, I was well into the script by the time I turned off the water. A bird chirped outside, and I decided *High Midnight* wasn't so bad. I finished it forty minutes later and ran some more hot water for an extra shave.

High Midnight was about a middle-aged former sheriff who shoots his wife and her lover and then holes up on a hill at the far end of town with his dog. Angered because no one told him what was going on behind his back, the former sheriff keeps the town pinned down. The easygoing present sheriff tries everything he can think of to get the old sheriff down. He sends an Indian killer, mounts a charge and when the town begins to talk about getting rid of him, the new sheriff offers to meet the old sheriff in a shoot-out, though the old sheriff is a former gunfighter and the present one an inexperienced novice. Before the shoot-out takes place, the old sheriff accuses the new one of having been one of those his wife had taken up with. The new sheriff says yes, but adds that he was just one of many. In the shoot-out the old sheriff, who has been suffering from a wound from one of the attacks on him, misses and is killed though he wounds the new sheriff, who in a final speech says the old boy was wrong but he stuck by his principles. The new sheriff then throws down his badge because the town has not supported him and rides wounded out of town.

I wasn't sure whether Cooper was going to be the old or the new sheriff. It was a cinch Tall Mickey Fargo would be a joke in either role, and the only thing for Lola was the part of the wife, who gets killed at the beginning of the picture but who appears in some flashbacks.

Withered and dry, I went to my room, pulled the mattress from my bed, lay on my back and fell asleep. I dreamed, as I frequently do, of Cincinnati, where I have never been. Nothing much ever happens to me in Cincinnati. I wander empty neighborhoods and feel lonely. Gradually I feel scared and wonder where the people are. Then a crane with a demolition ball comes down the street, and I hide in an empty building. It isn't a pleasant dream. My pleasant dreams are about Koko the Clown, but Koko won't come when bidden. He reserves his dream appearance for times of crisis.

When I woke up, the room was dark. I sat up, staggered to the lamp, turned it on and checked my watch. The hour hand hung limp. The minute hand said it was fifteen minutes to something. My Beech-nut clock said nine-fifty and my Arvin radio picked up the tail end of Bob Burns on KNX, so

I knew it was almost ten. Putting on my suit and a clean but frayed shirt with a tie which my nephews had given me for my birthday, I sneaked down the stairs, trying to avoid Mrs. Plaut. I failed. She caught me at the door.

"Mr. Peelers, Mr. Peelers," she cried, hurrying to me with short little steps and her hands up. "You had a call. Carole Lombard called and said to tell you to remember to tell Cary Grant to be reasonable."

"Thank you, Mrs. Plaut," I said.

"I will," she said with a smile, turning back into her parlor.

My decoding of the message was that Lombardi had called or had someone call to remind me to be sure Cooper agreed to make the picture. He was certainly determined.

It was almost eleven when I parked in front of the Big Bear Bar in Burbank. The street was quiet. A few lights were on in the nearby houses, and the lawns were creaking with crickets. Three cars were parked in front of or near the bar, and I thought I recognized one of them. When I got to the door, I could hear Lola Farmer belting "Rosie the Riveter." She should have stuck to ballads. I waited till she was finished before stepping in.

There was a bartender with the face of an orangutan serving a customer with the body of a chimp. At one of the tables a couple sat arguing in low voices. At another table sat someone I wasn't looking for, the squat man with the high voice who had laid me out in front of Mrs. Plaut's. At the table next to him sat the person I wanted, Shelly Minck. His back was to me, but I couldn't mistake that shape, that bald head and the cigar smoke. Lola was clinking the keys to think up another song. She looked about the same as she had in the afternoon, which was fine with me.

"Requests?" she asked.

"*The Man I Love,*" I said, and she looked up and gave me a smile of agony.

Shelly turned as quickly as he could at hearing my voice. He started to rise, but I got to him before he could get up and put my hand on his shoulder.

"It's not polite to leave when the lady starts a song," I whispered.

"I can explain," he said.

I winked at the squat man, who drank his beer and pretended not to see me.

"After the song," I told Shelly.

Lola did a reasonable job, considering the state of the piano and the limits of her voice. There was something so damned sad about her singing that I was beginning to like it.

I applauded and so did Shelly and the chimp at the bar. The arguing couple was too busy and the squat muscleman was still pretending not to be there. I waved to him to catch his attention, which caused him to rise, pay his bill and leave. His place was taken by the two men who had come through the door, Costello and Marco, both looking as if they could use the sleep I had taken.

"Talk, Shelly," I said, before Lola could start another song.

"It's like this . . ." he began, but I had had enough.

"No, on second thought don't talk. Just pay for your drink and get out, and stay out of this case."

"But . . ."

"Out," I shouted. Everyone looked at us, and I raised my hand to show it was just a friendly discussion between friends.

"I could help you, Toby," whined Shelly, pushing his glasses back from a nose that looked as if it had been immersed in mineral oil. I reached for his jacket, and he held up his right hand.

"All right, all right. I know when I'm not wanted."

"No you don't, Shel. That's the problem."

He got up, paid his bill and went out the door. Marco

and Costello had a discussion, probably considering if one of them should follow Shelly to see who he was and what I had to do with him. Marco got up and ambled out.

Lola played, sang and drank for about fifteen more minutes till the couple in battle got up and paid their bill. Then she took a break and came over to my table.

"Nice," I said.

"A few centuries ago I remember promising you a drink," she said, looking at me. "Jimmy," she called, and then to me, "What'll you have?"

I drank a beer when it came and looked at her with sympathy and more.

"The drink is all I promised," she said hoarsely.

"The drink is all you promised," I agreed, looking over at Costello, who was nursing a second beer.

"I'm going to be lucky to make it back to my place and into bed alone. It's been a tough day." She finished her drink and looked into the bottom of the glass.

"I understand," I said. "You need a ride?"

"Just a ride," she said, looking at me. From a distance she had looked all right, but close up I could see that dancing of the eyeballs that shows someone who might have trouble navigating the length of a napkin.

"Gotta get back to work," she said, standing, steadying herself and making it back to the piano. She ran a handful of fingers through her hair, coughed and began to sing. The monkey at the bar left in about ten minutes. That left just Costello, me and the barkeep. Lola wrapped up a medley of Cole Porter without losing too many words, and I clapped. I gave Costello a dirty look, and he joined in clapping. Jimmy the bartender was already cleaning up for the night.

"You need anything?" I asked Lola at the piano.

"A steady arm and a new head," she said and smiled, reaching under the piano for a small purse.

She said good night to the bartender, and I put my arm

around her to give her support to the door. I nodded to Costello that it was time to go. He caught me at the door and grabbed my arm.

"I gotta wait for Marco. He took the car."

"I'm not staying to keep you company." I told him and went out into the Burbank night with Lola. Somewhere a dog barked. The street was dark and quiet, and so was Lola.

She almost fell asleep on the way to the Glendale address she gave me. I knew the way. I grew up in Glendale. At least I got older in Glendale.

Her furnished apartment was in a new war boom building on the commercial strip. Some people were sitting outside swapping songs, lies and stories, waiting for the factory shifts to change or unwinding after a long day. I got Lola through the hall with writing on the walls. There was no carpeting and no attempt to cover the cement blocks which the building was made of. Our footsteps bounced around, and the few words I said were lost in echoes.

At her door she found her key and turned to me.

"I wouldn't be much good," she said with a sad smile.

"Some other time," I said wittily.

She touched my cheek and kissed me, her mouth soft and tired and tasting of sweet bourbon and lost dreams. I lost myself in the kiss, and then she pulled away.

"Like a teenage date," she said, and then she disappeared through the door, closing it behind her.

I felt sorry for myself. Someone was trying to kill me, but that wasn't what was making me sad. Ann was getting married. Carmen worked late and fought me off and Lola Farmer was too drunk and sad.

Heliotrope was quiet. Lights were out on the street, and Mrs. Plaut had long since tucked away her manuscript. I parked behind a Packard right in front of the house. It looked like Marco and Costello's Packard. I checked the license plate and it sounded right. Marco wasn't in the car.

No one stirred as I went into the house and up the stairs

to my room. I went in quietly and turned on my lights. Costello was sitting at my table, looking up at me with his eyes wide and his mouth open.

"Okay," I started to say wearily and then stopped. Something red trickled from Costello's mouth.

When I reached him, I could see the glassy look of pain and surprise in his eyes. One reason for it was the knife in his back. It was a long knife. Now you might wonder how I would know it was a long knife if it was imbedded in the back of my uninvited guest. It was my knife, one of the two kitchen knives that had come with the room.

"Who did it?" I asked, kneeling next to Costello, who grasped my arm with the grip of death.

"He . . ." gasped Costello.

"Who?"

"Yes . . . He . . . No . . . Yes," he whispered.

"Yes, no, yes?" I repeated.

"He . . . No . . . Yes," agreed Costello.

With that enlightening exchange, my guest fell over on his face, just missing a spot of milk I had failed to clean up from breakfast. He was dead. I knew what I had to do. Costello was short, but too heavy to haul away, and I didn't want to be caught trying. I could just let him sit there till morning and then call the police, but I didn't think I'd get much sleep, and besides it would just be putting off the inevitable.

I went to the hall phone and called the Wilshire Police District Office. It wasn't quite in this area, but that's where my brother Phil was in charge of homicide.

Phil wasn't at the station: The sergeant on the desk said he'd give me Officer Cawelti. I said no thanks. Cawelti and I were not sleep-over friends.

I called Phil at home. His wife Ruth answered sleepily.

"Ruth, this is Toby. Did I wake you?"

"No, what time is it? The baby's up with something. What's wrong, Toby?"

Before I could say more I could hear a grunt and the

bouncing of springs. Behind that was the cry of my niece Lucy.

"Toby," came Phil's voice, wavering between concern and anger, "what do you want?"

"I've got something for the boys," I said softly. "I picked up autographs of Babe Ruth, Bill Dickey, Mark Koenig and Bob Meusel this morning."

"You're drunk," hissed Phil.

"I've also got something for you–your favorite–a corpse."

"Where?" he said soberly.

"Here, in my room."

"You did it?" asked Phil seriously.

"No, someone left him as a present."

"I'll be there in half an hour."

While I waited for Phil I went carefully through Costello's pockets. They didn't tell me much except that his last name was Santucci, that he was from Chicago and that he was married. He had forty bucks and a holster with a gun which hadn't been fired. I thought over his nonsense comments and tried to make sense of them. I woke Gunther, who came in wearing a tiny gray bathrobe with a sash. Gunther avoided examining the corpse and told me that he had heard some noises in my room about an hour earlier, but that since I hadn't answered when he knocked, he had assumed I was all right.

I told Gunther about my conversation a few minutes ago with the now-dead Costello, and Gunther listened seriously, touched his tiny chin and hurried to his room for a pencil and paper.

"I think I understand," he said animatedly. "You asked him who killed him and he said . . ."

"He. No. Yes," I finished, looking at Costello's head.

"Okay," I went on, wanting to make a Spam sandwich but thinking it might look bad if my brother came while I was munching over the corpse. "He was killed by He. Yes. No Yes."

Is there a street perhaps or a place in Los Angeles called Yesno or Yezno or Yeznoyes or . . ."

"That's it, Gunther," I said, pointing a finger at him. "No Yes. Noyes. There is a street called Noyes in Burbank, and that's where I was tonight. Costello didn't know how to pronounce it. Maybe he was telling us where he was killed, not who killed him. So what do we have?"

You have," explained Gunther, "a man who was murdered on Noyes Street."

I don't see what difference where he was killed makes. But that's my knife in his back. Either the killer came here earlier and took it, or he got Costello here somehow and killed him. Either way he was dumped here to get me in trouble and out of a case I'm on."

There was a loud knock at the door downstairs.

Phil," I said, and Gunther put his hands in his robe and hurried back to his room. He had no affection for Phil, and Phil in a bad mood would think nothing of drop-kicking Gunther through the window.

There was no chance that Mrs. Plaut would hear the door no matter how hard Phil pounded. I ran down and opened it.

Phil Pevsner, brother of Tobias Leo Pevsner who at an early age became Toby Peters, was a little taller than me, a little broader, a few years older and much heavier. His hair was close-cut, curly and the color of steel. His thick, strong fingers scratched constantly from habit; dandruff or perplexity, I've never been sure. He started doing it in 1918 when he came back from the war. Phil hadn't even bothered with the tie he usually kept unmade around his neck. Behind him stood Sergeant Steve Seidman, a cadaverous man who had little to say and was my brother's partner. Seidman was a strange creature, a man who actually liked my brother.

"Where is it?" Phil said through his teeth.

I handed him the crumpled sheet with the Yankee autographs. He crushed it in his fist and was about to fling it in my face.

"They're real," I said, holding up my hands. "For Dave and Nate."

He shoved the paper into his pocket and pushed me out of the way. Seidman followed behind, giving me a shake of his head to show me he disapproved of my not growing up.

In my room, we stood looking down at Costello solemnly for a few seconds before Phil sighed and Seidman began to examine the body.

"Now," said Phil, grabbing my shirt and looking into my eyes, "start talking–fast, clear and straight."

Phil hated crime just a little more than he hated me. His impulse was to smash a hole through criminals and brothers and make straight for whatever sunlight and peace might be on the other side. Sometimes I thought Phil might have a few screws rattling around in his head. For more than twenty-five years he had been trying to clean up Los Angeles. The more he cleaned up and the more criminals he found, the more corpses came. At one point he had even charged a two-bit gunman with picking wildflowers, a crime punishable in Los Angeles by a $200 fine and up to six months in jail. There was no end to being a cop, and that frustrated him. Since he could never really win, he hated each new murderer and victim, who reminded him that things were getting worse instead of better, that Phil Pevsner would not make it a better world for his three kids. Since I seemed to be in the business of bringing him more business, I was not one of his favorite Californians.

"I don't know his name," I said. "He's from Chicago, a minor hood. A case I'm on has something to do with a guy named Lombardi, who just came here from the East to start a sausage factory."

"A case?" said Phil evenly. "Tell me more about it."

"Client," I said and smiled. "I have to check with the client."

"How many times did I tell you there is no such thing for private detectives? You're not a priest or a lawyer. Sam Spade was full of shit." Phil shook me around a little to see if sense would find an accidental resting place in my head. It wouldn't.

"I'm not talking about the law," I said. "I'm talking about ethics."

Phil laughed. I didn't like the laugh. I think he was getting ready to go for the long-distance Toby-throwing record. So I talked fast.

"This guy and another Chicago hood named Marco were tailing me. They picked me up yesterday and they've been on my tail since."

"So you got upset and skewered one of them when he came to lean on you," Phil explained.

"No," I said. "I was out for the night at a bar in Burbank. You can check at the bar. It wasn't crowded."

"That's not proof of anything, and you know it," shouted Phil. "You recognize the knife?"

"Which knife?" I said innocently.

"The one in the guy's back, you smartass piece of . . ." If I had enough nose left for him to break, he would have done it. Seidman put a hand on his shoulder and stepped between us. Phil backed off, his face red, his teeth grinding.

"Back off, Toby," Seidman whispered. He had seen this game of bait-the-brother between me and Phil before. He had tried to figure it out and had tried to reason with both of us, me to stop needling Phil and Phil to stop taking the hook. The Pevsner brothers are a proud and foolish lot. We have no interest in listening to reason.

"You think you can keep from driving him to kill you while I call the evidence boys and the coroner?" Seidman said, looking over at Phil, who was glaring angrily at the corpse.

"Okay," I said, and Seidman went out to use the hall phone.

With his back to me, Phil said, "Did he say anything before he died?"

"Only Mother of Mercy, is this the end of Costello," I said.

Phil didn't turn. I think he was trying to count to ten.

"On the head of my wife and kids," he said with a calmness that scared even me, "if you give me one more wise-ass answer tonight, I'll maim you."

He had done it before. It was time for me to cut the comments and stick to lies and near-facts. I wasn't sure if it was in me. My brain is trickier than I am and makes me say things that aren't always healthy for either of us.

"Maybe your client did this?" Phil tried.

"Nope," I said, moving to the sofa to sit and being careful not to touch Mrs. Plaut's doilies. I noticed for the first time that if you looked at the doily long enough, you could see the face of Harold Ickes in the pattern. "In a crazy way, old Costello here and my client were after the same thing. There is a guy whose name I don't know who looks like a file cabinet. He–"

"No name . . . ?" said Phil, adding, "You got a clean glass?"

I found him a glass, and he filled it with water and took a white pill from a bottle in his coat. I knew better than to ask what it was.

"What was that?" I asked, even though I knew better.

"Anti-Toby pills," he said, rubbing his fingers over his gray stubble of morning beard. Seidman came back. His face showed nothing. It never did, but his eyes went to both of us to be sure that we had survived a minute or two alone together.

"They'll be here in fifteen, twenty minutes."

There was a knock on the door and Seidman opened it to Mrs. Plaut, who came in clutching her robe around her with one hand and holding a lug wrench in the other.

"Are you in need of assistance, Mister Peelers?" she said, looking with suspicion at Phil and Seidman.

"No, thank you, Mrs. Plaut," I said. "These are policemen. There's been an accident."

Then her eyes caught sight of the body slumped over with the knife in his back.

"You call that an accident?" she said. "There is no way anyone can get accidentally stabbed in the back. And that's my knife. Mr. Peelers, that knife will have to be thoroughly cleaned or replaced."

"It will be, Mrs. Plaut," I said reassuringly, ushering her back out the door. She seemed to be hearing much better in the hours before dawn.

"I didn't think you were that kind of exterminator," she whispered to me in the hall.

"I'm not," I said as she turned her back. She put the wrench over her shoulder and went down the stairs.

"Your knife," said Phil when I came back in.

"I didn't recognize it," I said.

"We're going to my office," said Phil. It wasn't an invitation. When the evidence men came, Phil and I got in his car. Seidman stayed behind to interview people in the boarding house and neighborhood who might have seen something.

Phil and I said nothing all the way to the Wilshire station. When we got inside, Phil didn't bother to greet the old sergeant on duty, and when we got upstairs, the only ones in the detective squad room were a cleaning woman and Cawelti, a guy with tight clothes, a smirk and hair parted down the middle and plastered like a Gay Nineties bartender. We waded through the day's garbage and into Phil's office, where he sat heavily in his chair behind the desk. I sat in the chair opposite him. We looked at each other for a few minutes, and for the first time I realized that Phil's office was about the same size as my office. Not only that—he had laid it out the same way mine was, even down to his cop diploma on the wall and a photograph, only the photograph was of his wife and kids. I tried to remember whose office had come first. I thought it was his. I considered pointing out the resemblance we both had missed, but Phil picked up his phone.

"Get me two coffees," he barked. The person on the other end, who I assumed was Cawelti, said something and Phil nodded politely before continuing. "That's a sad story, John. I don't care if you have to run down to the drugstore and break in. I want *you* to be in my office with two coffees within ten minutes or I'll give you a coffee enema." He hung up, ever the master of the colorful vulgarism.

"Pa wanted you to be a lawyer," he said out of nowhere.

"I didn't want to be a lawyer," I said. "I liked my hands in my own pockets." I'd read that somewhere, but I didn't know the source and was sure Phil wouldn't.

"You could have been a police officer. You were . . ." He stopped. We had been through this and it got us nowhere. He reached into his drawer and found a pad of paper. He reached deeper and found a pencil. He shoved them both to me and told me to write out a report, the whole thing. He didn't even say "or else."

I asked Phil what time it was.

"You've got a watch," he growled.

"Pa's watch," I explained. Phil told me it was three in the morning.

I pulled out the card Cooper had given me and called the number while Phil stared at me.

"Huh?" came Cooper's sleepy voice.

"This is Toby Peters. We've got a complication." I explained what had happened without giving anything away to

Phil and hoped that Cooper hadn't fallen asleep. Then I concluded, "I think I should tell them about your involvement and ask for their discretion."

"I don't like it," said Cooper finally.

"I'm not throwing a party over the whole thing myself," I said.

"A man has to do what a man has to do," said Cooper. "I say things like that in my movies but I don't know what they really mean. So you do what you have to as long as I don't have to back it up in public."

I hung up and began the report. I was just finishing when Cawelti brought in the coffee. He was not happy about bringing in the coffee. He was not happy about seeing me.

"Thanks, John," Phil said.

"Thanks, John," I added, and Cawelti left, slamming the door behind him.

The coffee was cold, but it was coffee. My report was all truth. I left out a lot, but what was in there was bonded stuff that would hold up.

"Do I get a ride home?" I said.

"It's a nice morning," said Phil, finishing his coffee. "You can take a streetcar or taxi. It will give you some time to think and us some time to tidy up your room."

I said thanks and went into the squad room. Cawelti was gone, but the cleaning lady had accumulated a shoulder-high pile of rubble.

"You a cop?" she said in a pretty good Marjorie Main imitation.

"No," I said.

"You'd be surprised at the junk I find in here sometimes," she said, starting to shovel her pile into a barrel on wheels. "Found an ear once," she said. "How can you lose an ear?"

I left her musing on life as I went out and into the first chill hint of dawn. I didn't have to walk home, as it turned out. I went half a block toward the drugstore, from where I planned to call a cab, when a car pulled along next to me and Marco looked out and back at the station.

"Get in," he said.

"I think I'll walk," I said. "Fresh air will do me good."

"Get in," he insisted, showing his gun. "In back."

"We're half a block from the police station," I reminded him.

"And you're a few seconds from termination, if you don't get in," he said.

I liked his reasoning and got into the back seat. I wasn't alone. Lombardi sat with one hand rubbing the bridge of his nose. He had a headache, and it was probably me.

"Our friends from Chicago are very upset at this turn of events," Lombardi said softly. "And I am not pleased, either. We understand that Mr. Santucci has been murdered."

Marco squirmed in the front seat and nearly whimpered, "What do I tell my wife? He is supposed to be breaking me into the business and he gets killed. How do you think she'll feel after what happened to her brother?"

"Bad?" I guessed.

"We all regret this shocking tragedy," said Lombardi. "Now, you must first convince us that you are not responsible. Our colleague is killed in your room with your knife. He was following you."

"How do you know about the knife?"

"I have a headache," Lombardi said. "Talk very quietly, very quietly. I have a friend in the police department. Actually, it is the friend of a friend. That's all you have to know. On the other hand, there is so much a person in my position has to know. Being a businessman is not as easy as many people think. One has responsibilities."

"I didn't kill him," I said softly. "Look, someone is still trying to get rid of me. Someone who took a couple of shots at me today. He's the guy we should all be looking for. Him and whoever hired him."

"I must be quite disoriented from my headache," Lombardi said, "because what you are saying makes sense. I think you should find this person or persons and quietly stop them."

"Wait," growled Marco.

"And," Lombardi continued, "if you come up with the name of someone who should be made quiet, especially the someone who did this terrible thing to our friend from Chicago, then you will tell me and the bereaved brother-in-law will speak to them. You of course understand. I haven't time to be more subtle. Here," he called to Marco.

Marco turned his huge face to us. "You mean we just let him go?"

"Yes," said Lombardi, "for now. Now go, Mr. Peters."

I got out, and the car pulled away. I was still about two miles from my room, but I had things to think about. I found an all-night grill I knew and ate a couple of bowls of Wheaties with a cup of coffee.

The grill always had a rear table full of guys who looked like truck drivers, but I had never seen any trucks parked on the street. Their conversation was usually about the war, food and the movie industry.

While I downed the dregs of my bowl and considered ordering another, a guy who looked and sounded like Lionel Stander shouted angrily at another mug, "What are you talking about? Bette Davis can act rings around her, rings around her. Joan Crawford got no range, no reserves of emotion to draw on, you moron."

The Joan Crawford advocate rose to the occasion and clenched his fists, countering, "Is that so? Crawford in *Rain* was superb, projected brass and pathos at the same time."

The two critics snarled at each other, and I got out before a brawl developed. My vote was for Olivia DeHavilland, but her name hadn't entered the conversation.

CHAPTER SIX

The body was gone when I got back to my room. I saw a few bloodstains, but I was too tired to tidy up. Mrs. Plaut had trapped me briefly. She wanted to know if I needed a new knife. I told her I would make do with my remaining sharp one.

I didn't bother to look in the mirror. I could feel the stubble on my chin and I knew it would be gray-brown and that I'd look like an overdone makeup job for a Warner Brothers gangster. I threw my coat on the sofa, kicked off my shoes, took off my shirt, wiggled my toes and plopped on the mattress.

When I woke up, I tried to hold onto a piece of dream, to pull it by the tail so I could see the whole thing. It had something to do with baseballs, and I think there were horses in it, but I couldn't rope it and it rode or flew away. It was nearly noon. My tabletop Arvin told me Japan had almost won in Java and Burma, but that we had retaliated by having the FBI arrest three Japanese in Sacramento. Supposedly the three Japanese had weapons and uniforms and were ready to attack the state capitol. John Barrymore had just turned sixty, and Ava Gardner was in Hollywood Hospital for an emergency appendectomy, with husband Mickey Rooney at her side.

I called the number Cooper had given me and got a woman who didn't identify herself. Cooper was out, and she didn't want to tell me where he was. I said it was a matter of life and death, mine and possibly his. I suggested she call him, get his okay and let me call her back.

Fifteen minutes later, after discovering that Gunther had gone out to visit a publisher, I washed, shaved, dressed, and consumed a Spam sandwich, and then I called them back. The woman told me Cooper was at Don the Beachcomber's in Hollywood, having lunch with his mother.

Ten minutes later I was in the semi-darkness of Don the Beachcomber's, which had opened in 1933 and seemed to be decorated for a Paramount South Sea Island picture. I told the waiter who I was and whom I was looking for and was escorted through the crowd. Cornel Wilde was talking intensely to a thin, dark man who had paused with his fork up to listen. I caught Wilde's voice saying, "So what choice do we have?" and was led beyond to a dark corner booth.

"Mr. Peters," Cooper said, gulping down a glob of lobster and half-rising, with his huge right hand out. I took his hand, and he said, "This is my mother."

"Mrs. Cooper," I said politely, taking the seat offered to me.

"Alice," she said. "Are you joining us for lunch, Mr. Peters?"

There was a touch of English accent in Alice Cooper and more than a touch of maternal watchfulness. For the first time since I had met him, the shy screen Cooper appeared with an almost bashful look at his mother and at me. She was in her sixties and bore little resemblance to her famous son, but son he was, and forty or not, she watched him eat as if she were ready to tell him to switch the fork to the other hand or chew more slowly.

"We'll talk business a little later," Cooper said to me with a slight raising of his right eyebrow, meant, I assumed, to tell me that his mother was to know nothing of what was going on.

"How about a drink?" Cooper said. "I suggest the Missionary's Downfall or the Pearl Diver." He kept on eating his double order of lobster as he talked. "The recipes for drinks here are kept secret. The bottles have numbers instead of labels so rivals can't copy them. Even the bartenders know the recipes by numbers. You know, half a jigger of 12, a little 7."

"Fascinating," I smiled, wanting to get on with business instead of watching Cooper eat.

"He got his appetite when he was sixteen," explained Alice Cooper proudly without taking her eyes from her son, who smiled with a cheekful. "My older boy Arthur joined the army in 1917, and my husband was busy at the capitol. All the Indian workers at the ranch went to war. Frank and I had to take care of five hundred head of cattle."

"Frank?"

Cooper raised his fork to indicate that he was Frank.

"My older brother went to war in 1917 too and left me with my father in a grocery store," I said, but Alice Cooper cared nothing for my war stories. She went on.

"We're from Montana, you know," she said. I nodded, accepting a cup of coffee from the waiter to keep my hands busy.

"I remember you that year, swinging an ax in twenty-below weather to break frozen hay bales," Cooper said with a grin, "and the two of us working our way through six-foot snow drifts to feed the cattle."

"When the year was over and Arthur came back," Alice Cooper went on, "Frank had grown thirteen inches and was six-foot-four."

"Six-three," corrected Cooper. "Paramount added that inch."

"Anyway, he came out of that year with a healthy appetite."

It was clear that she had long ago finished whatever her lunch had been and was sitting around admiring her son. Then she stood.

"It's almost one," she said as if an important decision had been made. "I've got to get back to the Judge."

"Tell Dad I'll see him before I leave," Cooper said, pausing in his consumption of the food reserves of the West Coast. "I told the driver where to take you."

Son dutifully kissed mother on the cheek, and mother shook my hand, saying it was nice to meet me and asking me to let her know what I thought could be done. I said I would and sat down as she left.

"Quite a woman," Cooper said, his sappy smile leaving him. He pointed at her and then himself. "She still thinks of me as a kid."

"What am I supposed to report to her about?" I said, looking around to see if Cornel Wilde was still there. He wasn't.

"I told her you were a surgeon," Cooper explained, buttering a roll and consuming it in polite pieces. "When I was in college, I had a pal named Harvey Markham. Harvey had polio as a kid and couldn't move his legs. His old man had altered a Model T for Harve. We drove around together. On one of our trips, Harve's hand brake failed at the top of a hill. I remember as if it were yesterday. The impact, the rolling over." Cooper's massive right hand rolled over to demonstrate.

"I got up and walked to the curb," he went on, looking around for something else to eat. "I wasn't dizzy or weak. My senses were sharpened. And then my left side failed me. It hung like a heavy dead thing and everything went blue. Harve was fine, but I woke up in a hospital. They said I had a broken leg and complications. I had to spend two years at Sunnyside–our ranch–where I did a lot of drawing and a lot of riding. I found out years later that the riding was the worst thing I could have done. I had a pelvic separation, and the riding made it worse. It's caused me misery ever since, and my mother keeps thinking she should have caught it back then. Every once in a while I tell her I'm seeing a new doctor to take care of it. So, what's on your mind?"

I told him in detail about Bowie, Gelhorn, Lola and the death of Costello. I told him about the man who had pounded me on the street and about Lombardi.

"I don't want to do the picture," said Cooper, downing a coffee. "*High Midnight*'s not a bad script. There'd have to be changes. I couldn't play the older sheriff–he's a killer–and the new sheriff's part isn't big enough. I can't break my contract, and I don't want to work with Gelhorn. But most of all," he said, tapping his finger on the table, "I don't want to be told what to do. I don't want to get you killed, and I don't want to get me killed, but . . ."

"There are some things a man can't walk away from," I finished.

Cooper grinned and said, "Something like that. What's your next move?"

"I think I have to go back to Lombardi," I said without joy.

Cooper looked around the room and sucked in his lower lip. He was wearing what looked like a brand new tweed jacket and striped tie with a gold stickpin.

"I'm supposed to go on a hunting trip with a friend up in Utah this afternoon, but I've got a few hours now. I'll go with you." He waved for the waiter.

"You don't have to," I said.

"I don't want to," Cooper said, signing the check, "but I see my father up there over my shoulder." He pointed up to his right shoulder. "And the Judge is telling me to go with you."

Cooper got up, and I joined him. Heads turned to look

at him as we left, and the sky greeted him outside by showing a touch of sun. By the time we got to my car, the sun had gone and the chill was back.

Lombardi's new sausage factory was on Washington Avenue, not far from Fourth. On a clear, quiet day I was sure you could hear the noise of Ocean Park a few miles away. The Coney Island of the West was quiet today.

Cooper and I parked in the same lot I had been driven to by the now-departed Costello and his word-logged brother-in-law. Construction workers were finishing off a wall outside and machines were being assembled inside when we went through the double doors. One of the guys installing a white slicing machine spotted Cooper and nudged his co-worker, who looked over at us. I moved deeper into the place with Cooper at my side, taking one long step for every two of mine.

In the storefront with its long counter, scale and display cases, we found Lombardi with his two helpers in white, making the place kosher-style. The one called Steve was the first to spot us. He nudged Lombardi, who turned around. I didn't like the look of anger that touched his face. I liked the smile that replaced it even less. He smoothed his hair with his left hand and offered his right to Cooper. Cooper took it.

"An honor to meet you," said Lombardi. Cooper said nothing. He had put on a steel look from some role in the past. "What can I do for you?"

"Mr. Cooper is not going to do *High Midnight,*" I said.

"I see," said Lombardi. "That's too bad. Too bad for maybe you and Mr. Cooper. There are certain influential people involved in this movie who will be very unhappy to hear that, very unhappy."

Lombardi looked at me for the first time. His smile grew on his marked face. "And you—you know that big mouth of yours is going to get you into a lot of trouble. I can think of lots of things to do with tongues that wag."

"Pickle them and sell them for thirty cents a pound sliced?" I tried.

"Something like that," he said. Then he turned to Cooper. "You know we have a mutual friend, Lola Farmer."

Now it was Cooper's turn to smile. "I've talked to Miss Farmer. If you're planning to let the newspapers know what happened back in 1933, go ahead. They've torn me up about Clara Bow and Lupe Velez and the Countess DeFrasso. You're talking about a long time ago."

"I understand there are other things besides our mutual friend that might make you consider this offer," Lombardi said, taking a step closer to Cooper. Cooper didn't back off. He met Lombardi's smile with his own through clenched teeth.

"Not . . . a . . . chance," Cooper said.

"We'll see, Mr. Big Brave Cowboy Star," hissed Lombardi.

There were a few seconds of silence, broken only by the sound of men in the next room grunting to install a machine.

"When you wanna call me that, smile," said Cooper with a massive, teeth-clenched grin.

Lombardi was no Walter Huston. He backed away, his smile fading and the look of hate returning.

"Get off our back," I said. "Tell your friends to get off our back. Find another star. Maybe Joel McCrea is free."

The two guys in white stepped forward toward us, ready to attack us with coils of Polish sausage.

"It doesn't end like this," said Lombardi.

"I think we'll all be better off and live longer if it does," I said, motioning to Cooper to back away. The place was crawling with workmen, so I was sure Lombardi wouldn't do anything. I wanted to give him time to think over what had taken place. If he was convinced that Cooper wouldn't take the role no matter what, he might pass it on to the ones who were pushing it. I hoped they'd see that there would be no percentage in giving Cooper a tough time. They'd have nothing to gain except a lot of trouble.

"You did that line well," I said to Cooper as we settled back into the car.

"Thanks," he said. "I've had a lot of practice. Do you go through this sort of thing a lot?"

"It happens," I said, heading for Pico Boulevard.

"They had me scared," he said. "I don't mind admitting it."

"You didn't show it," I said. "I was scared too. That's part of what makes it worthwhile. That touch of fear. It brings out the fact that you're living."

From the corner of my eye, I could see that Cooper was looking at me as if I were an alien life form. Then some touch of recognition appeared on his face. "I get something like that when I drive a fast car on a narrow road," he said. I nodded, and we were quiet for a while.

I explained that I thought the visit might convince Lombardi to lay off. There was no guarantee, but it had been worth the effort. Cooper gave me the name of the town in Utah where he was going for the next few days. I didn't write it down. I'd remember.

I dropped Cooper at the Goldwyn Studios, where he had an appointment with the people who were doing the wardrobe for the Gehrig movie. He reached through the car window to take my hand.

"Thanks," he said.

"My job and pleasure, Mr. Cooper," I said.

"Call me Coop," he returned and strode away.

My confidence in front of Cooper was not matched by my nagging questions. Someone had tried to kill me and had put my kitchen knife in Costello. Even if we had convinced Lombardi, and I doubted if we had, he might have no control over the squat man or any of the others who had an interest in seeing to it that Cooper made *High Midnight.*

I went back to the Farraday Building. Shelly was sitting in his own dental chair, eyes inches away from the dental journal in front of him. He heard me come in and leaped out of the chair, removing his cigar.

"Now, Toby," he said. "I can explain about last night."

"Forget it," I said, going past him and examining the coffee pot. It had something in it that looked like silt. I poured it into a cup that looked as if it had been cleaned within the decade. "Last night when you left the Big Bear Bar, a guy followed you, a big guy. Did you see him?"

Relieved, Shelly pushed his glasses back on his nose and said, "Right, yes, a big guy. I got into my car and he watched me. There wasn't anyplace to hide on the street. Then another guy who had been in the bar came up behind him."

"Squat guy, looked like a brick?"

"Right," beamed Shelly. "That was all I saw. I pulled away. They stayed there talking."

"Shel," I said, sipping the sludge, "that big guy's partner was killed last night, a knife in his back and his body left in my room. It could have been you. Maybe it should have been."

Shelly wiped his hands on his smock and looked at the door as if the killer were right behind me.

"Being a dentist may not be as exciting as being a detective," I said, pouring the rest of the glue into the spit sink, "but it is safer. Stick to the reconstruction of Mr. Stange's mouth. It will stand as a memorial to your true calling."

Shelly nodded morosely. I left him to think about it and went into my office to make a phone call or two. Call number one was to Mickey Fargo. There was no answer at what might have been a hall phone. I decided to try for him anyway. Shelly hid in his dental journal as I came out. We didn't talk.

Tall Mickey Fargo lived in a building on Normandie

not far from Slauson. The building was another one of those that were slapped up fast to absorb the people who were streaming into Los Angeles in spite of the war scare. The defense plants, airplane factories, boat yards and oil wells were promising easy money, and I knew how much people were willing to risk for easy money that seldom turned out to be so easy.

A guy about sixty-five or seventy and a woman the same age sat in wooden kitchen chairs on the front stoop of the building. I made my way through them and found Mickey's mailbox. The card on it read, Tall Mickey Fargo, King of Deadgulch. Mickey or someone had drawn a steer skull in the corner. There was no bell, but it was easy to find the right door. I knocked, half-expecting to get no answer and considering the easiest way to break in and look around. But a voice answered my knock, and I recognized it as Mickey Fargo's.

"Coming," he said, and a few seconds later the door opened.

He was wearing an old denim shirt and dark slacks. A big wide belt with a massive silver buckle tried to hold up his stomach.

"You're the guy who messed up my fall yesterday," he said, stepping back to let me in.

"Sorry," I said, accepting the invitation. "I didn't mean . . ."

"Hell," bellowed Fargo, his jowls bouncing merrily, "that's all right. Max says he got enough. Damned fall, though."

He limped into the room and pointed to a chair. I sat and looked around the room. The walls were filled with photographs of Fargo with men in cowboy suits. He watched me looking at the photos and said solemnly, "They're all there. I've worked with 'em all—Hoxie, Mix, Jones, both Maynards.

Hoot, Harry Carey. You name 'em, they shot me." He laughed, but something caught in his throat, and it turned to a gag. He hurried off red-faced for a glass of water.

He was back in two minutes or less, full of Western hospitality.

"What can I offer you and what can I do for you?" he said, easing into the chair opposite me.

"Nothing, thanks," I said. "You can talk to me about *High Midnight.*"

"Mind if I get a drink?" he said, grunting out of the chair and limping to a decrepit refrigerator in the corner. I wondered what the cowboy heroes looking down thought of the sagging furniture in the single room of their former nemesis. Fargo came back with a glass of something that could have been wine, rot-gut or flat Coke.

"Now," he said, settling in.

"You think you can sit still long enough for us to get through this conversation?" I asked, amiable. "I've got an appointment I've got to get to by next Wednesday."

A flash of red crept into Fargo's eyes. Maybe it had been there all the time, but it caught something of his old screen villainy. I didn't think he was capable of holding it for a whole scene. I was right. The effort of looking angry took too much out of him. His face twitched, gave in and sagged.

"You've got no call coming in here and talking like this," he said, sipping his drink.

"You're right. I've been rude. I apologize. Did you pay someone to try to force Gary Cooper to take the *High Midnight* role?" I said, being even more rude.

Fargo could take it as well as he had taken a fake punch from Tom Mix. He just sipped his drink and shrugged.

"Why would I do that?" he said.

"Because you want this movie, and there isn't going to be a movie without Cooper," I explained.

"Look around you," he said, waving his drink at the

furniture. "Does it look like I could afford to hire anybody to do something like that?"

"A friend, maybe," I tried.

"Who are you, and what do you want?" he said, considering an indignant rise from his seat.

I went through the whole explanation about Shelly impersonating me and Cooper getting threatened and Costello getting killed.

"I want the picture," said Fargo. "That's a fact, but I'm not about to do anyone in for it, and if I was I wouldn't have to do any hiring. I'd do it myself. I've put on a few pounds, but I can still use my hands, and I can still shoot. I remember one time Tom Tyler and I had–"

"Why does Gelhorn want you in *High Midnight*?" I interrupted.

Fargo took another drink and looked off into the corner for another excuse to leave and gather what passed for thoughts. "We go way back, Max and me," he said. "I respect him as a director, and he respects me as an actor. He knows I can take off fifteen, twenty pounds, get in shape for this."

It would have taken more like forty pounds to make Tall Mickey Fargo look tall again, and I just didn't think the mass in front of me had the will to do it. Fargo couldn't handle either of the two major roles in the film. He might make it as the friendly blacksmith in one scene, but that wasn't what he was talking about.

"What have you got on Gelhorn or whoever is backing Gelhorn?" I said.

"That'll just about do it," he said, working his way to a standing position. "You got ten seconds to get out of here and stay out."

I had expected something more colorful from an old Western villain, something like, this closet isn't big enough for both of us. There was no way Fargo could have thrown me out of the room, but I had no reason to humiliate him. My goal had been to provoke him a little and get a feeling about him. I had provoked him, but I wasn't sure of the feeling.

"I'm going, partner," I said, taking a quick step to the door so he wouldn't have to be forced to try to throw me out. "Just think about what I said. I'll be back."

My next stop was Max Gelhorn's office. It was getting a little late in the day, but I didn't want another shot fired at me if I could head it off.

The chunky girl with the running nose and box of Kleenex looked up at me suspiciously when I went through the door of Max Gelhorn Productions.

"You are not Mr. Fligdish of the Fourth Commercial Bank," she said accusingly.

"I am not," I confessed. "I'm a pederast."

She looked at me, puzzled, with bulbous cheeks that seemed to be concealing apples.

Gelhorn was watching the exchange from inside his office. He stood up behind his desk and shouted, "What the hell do you want? Didn't you do enough yesterday?"

"Hey," I said in as friendly a manner as I could, "remember I'm the one who works for Gary Cooper and you're the one who wants him."

"There are limits," shouted Gelhorn, rubbing his cheek.

"Are there?"

"Come in," Gelhorn grumbled, sitting again. I went around the secretary's desk. She tried to muster a sneeze to aim in my direction but it didn't come. I squeezed into Gelhorn's office, past piles of scripts and stacks of trade papers. His desk was cluttered with photographs, more scripts and assorted props.

"Have a seat," he said. He bobbed nervously behind his desk, touched a script, straightened it out and looked at me. I sat.

"Well?" he said.

"Not very," said I.

"Hey, I can do without this dialogue. It's bad enough I have to direct it. I don't have to listen to this crap in my own office. Just talk straight and back to business."

I took my time and admired a poster on the wall of an old Western that Gelhorn had produced and directed. The star was Kermit Maynard, and Tall Mickey Fargo was about the fifth name down the cast list. Kermit was pointing a gun out of the poster in my general direction. Kermit's face was a silly pink.

"Where in your wildest dreams did you get the idea that Gary Cooper would agree to make *High Midnight* with you?" I said.

Gelhorn rose and pointed the closest thing he could find at me. It was a reel of film. The tail of the film unraveled and dribbled onto the floor.

"Look, you," said Gelhorn, *High Midnight* is a good script and . . ."

". . . and the only way you stood a rat's chance of getting Cooper was if you scared or blackmailed him into it," I finished.

"No," he said, trying to gain his composure and rewind the film, which was unraveling at a wild pace. He dropped the whole mess on the floor. "I had Lola Farmer's assurance that she could talk Cooper into it, that they were old friends. I had a good script. I had good money behind it, enough to make Cooper a good offer. He won't be sorry if he makes this picture."

"Max," I sighed, "you know this business well enough to know that Cooper is under contract to Goldwyn."

"He can get out for a picture if he wants to," Gelhorn said, sitting and starting to sulk. "He's gotten his way before, getting conveniently sick to raise his salary or get out of a picture he didn't like."

"But he doesn't want to do *High Midnight,"* I repeated slowly, as if I were talking to an idiot.

Gelhorn didn't hear or didn't want to hear. A plea entered his voice. "Some people behind this aren't happy with Cooper."

"So they tried to kill me and maybe got rid of someone who was protecting me or looked as if he was. All a little warning to Cooper to give in."

"For Christ's sake," laughed Gelhorn in hysteria. "Killing people to make a movie? Are you out of your mind?"

"It's been done," I said, looking at Kermit Maynard for support.

"I didn't kill anyone or have anyone killed or order anyone to kill or . . ."

"You know a squat guy with a high voice?" I said.

"Lots of them. Casting books full of them," he said. "You making a movie?"

"No, looking for a killer." I got up. "How's the horse?"

"He'll recover, thank God. I think our interview is over," said Gelhorn. "Miss Lloyd, please show Mr. Peters the way out."

"If I take a step backward, I'll be out," I said.

"Then," said Gelhorn, "take a step backward by all means."

Miss Lloyd lumbered behind me, spreading germs. I eased past her, got a last look at Gelhorn's glaring eyes and left the premises of Max Gelhorn Productions. Things were making a little sense. I needed the squat man to put it together. Sooner or later he'd find me.

I made a few stops. First I went to Levy's to have a sandwich and a cup of coffee and tell Carmen the cashier sweet things. She was a buxom widow who made a pastime of frustrating me. She never quite said no, but something always managed to keep us from getting together.

"You're really working for Gary Cooper?" she said

while ringing up the bill on an early diner. The diner tried not to show that he was listening to our conversation. He was a thin guy with no chin.

"Cross my navel," I said. "He's been fooling around with a wrestler named Crusher Morgan. They want to get married, but Crusher's wife won't let him go. I'm trying to talk Crusher's wife into letting the mug go so he and Cooper can go away together."

The diner wanted to stay to hear more, but he had no excuse. He had to depart to retell the tale or maybe savor the secret knowledge for the rest of his days.

"Why do you do things like that?" said Carmen, lifting the corner of her mouth.

"I don't know," I said seriously. "It just comes out. We still on for the fights tomorrow night?"

"We're on," she smiled. I reached over and touched her hand. It was dark and a little rough.

"The manager's giving me a sour look," she said, glancing over my shoulder.

I took the hint and departed, stopping only at the A & P, unable to resist the sign in the window that said Ann Page Spaghetti was on sale, two 1-pound cans for 13 cents. When I got back to my rooming house, A & P treasure in hand, I was musing over ways to lure the squat man out for another try at me so I could trap him. Everything I could think of was dangerous.

Mrs. Plaut was nowhere in sight. Gunther's room was silent. I guessed that it was around six. The day was dark, but the sun was still there.

My first reaction when I entered my room was that the cops had finished with Costello's body and had returned it to me, but it wasn't Santucci lying over my table. Even from a bad angle, I had a good idea of who it was. I closed the door behind me, went to the table, put down the package and tried to convince myself that this hadn't happened before. I could see now that it was the squat man, his high voice stilled for good. A knife was in his back, a little higher than the one that had been in Costello, but just as deadly. It was also my knife. I was now out of sharp knives.

I did the only sane thing I could do. I put a chair in front of my door to keep out sudden visitors and sat down to a bowl of Post Toasties with milk and sugar. I kept looking at the body, hoping it would tell me something. I didn't taste the cereal. Only then did I go through his pockets and find nothing. Someone had taken his wallet. I had the feeling the police would not accept this as a routine robbery.

If I could have carried him, I might have lugged him to my car and dropped him in Barnsdall Park under an olive tree. I might get caught, but it would have been better than having the police find me here with my second body in as many days. It was then that the knock came at the door. I had been too busy trying to get some information out of the corpse by simply staring at him to hear the footsteps.

"I'm sick," I said. "Come back later."

"It's the police, Peters," came the unpleasant but familiar voice of Officer Cawelti.

"My clothes are off," I said.

"Open the damn door," he shouted, "or we'll kick it in."

"You have a warrant?" I said, considering someplace to hide a big body in a small room.

"I don't need a warrant," he yelled. "I have reason to believe a felony is in progress in there."

"You got a friendly phone call," I said, walking to the door. He was already pushing at it when I removed the chair. Cawelti came skidding in, his gun out. An old cop in uniform was right behind him with his gun out.

"Aha!" Cawelti grinned evilly, spotting the corpse.

"Very good," I said. "You spotted him right away. Excellent police work."

"Make jokes, you son of a bitch," he said as he laughed

with dancing eyes. "Now I've got you. You're running a goddamn butcher shop and your brother isn't going to get you out of this one."

"You want a confession?" I said. The uniformed cop had crossed over to the squat man to be sure he was dead. He nodded to Cawelti.

"You want to confess?" Cawelti said, a bead of joyful sweat forming on his brow.

"Come on, I didn't kill him. Who do you think called you?"

"A citizen doing his duty. Maybe your accomplice, who had a rush of guilty conscience. I don't give a turkey's toe," gloated Cawelti, indicating with his gun that he wanted me to turn around. I turned around and I knew he was pulling out his handcuffs.

"Hands behind your back," he said.

The old cop was going through the corpse's pockets. I knew Cawelti had to be looking at my wrists. I turned as fast as I could, chopping at his left arm in the hope that he had shifted the gun so he could put the cuffs on with his right hand. I was right. The gun sailed across the room and hit the old cop. I shoved Cawelti back, and he tumbled over my mattress on the floor.

"Now hold it," ordered the old cop, reaching for the gun he had put away, but I went for the door and was out with no shot behind me. I could hear them scrambling as I went down the stairs three at a time. Mrs. Plaut was on the porch, looking up at the sky.

"Beautiful crisp night," she said.

"Beautiful," I said, dashing down the stairs into it.

"Is there a problem, Mr. Peelers?" she shouted as I ran down the street. I could hear Cawelti thunder onto the steps behind me.

"Stop," he shouted, which struck me as a stupid thing to say, but what choice did he have. I didn't stop. I got to my car and pulled away just as Cawelti, his plastered hair hanging over his eyes, raised his gun and took a shot at me. The bullet hit the top of the Buick and raced into the early evening. He shouldn't have been shooting at me on a residential street, but he didn't care. For all I know, the next shot probably killed an innocent stroller. I went around the corner and headed for Melrose Avenue.

I had to admire whoever was knocking off the hoodlums in Los Angeles. I didn't think they were doing it as a civic duty, but they were managing quite a bit, including getting me in boiling oil over my not-too-tall head. They or he or she had also taken away my best suspect and reduced my culinary wares.

Now the police were after me. A killer might still be after me. It was like Robert Donat in *The 39 Steps.* All I needed was Alfred Hitchcock behind me to tell me what to do. Without Hitchcock, all I could think of was to drive fast, drive far and think about it later. A nagging voice that may have been my old man's was whispering somewhere, saying, "Call your brother." I didn't want to hear that voice. I preferred the other voice that said, "You have to find the killer now and prove your innocence."

Yep, that was the voice I would listen to, the Hitchcock voice; but the question was how was I going to do it. What I needed was a friend. I also needed a couple of tacos to settle my stomach. I stopped for the tacos, found a dime and made a phone call.

"It's me," I said.

"No," said Ann.

"I'm in trouble," I said.

"No," she said. "You're always in trouble. You like to be in trouble." She hung up. I knew she would. I drove to Burbank and parked a block away from the Big Bear Bar with my lights out. I slumped down. The street was clear. I got out and walked past with my collar up. I could hear

Lola's off-key sad voice inside, so I kept walking, went all the way around the block and got back in the car after I put a little mud on the plates. I could have used a cup of coffee or a good pillow or a new brain.

Darkness had come. I curled out of sight, determined to keep an alert watch for Lola. Vigilance was my watchword. I fell asleep almost instantly.

CHAPTER SEVEN

The cop was rapping at my car window with white knuckles, and the sunlight of morning crept around him. I had slept through the night and missed Lola's exit. I rolled down my window.

"What are you doing here, fella?" he said softly.

I sat up, tried to force my eyes open wide and touched my chin, which bristled for a shave I couldn't give it.

"My wife," I said, trying to find a sob. "I followed her and my best friend to that bar last night. I was waiting for them to come out. Must have fallen asleep."

"What were you planning to do when your wife and friend came out?" the cop said, examining the interior of the car.

"Follow them," I said. "Confront them. I don't know." I looked up at the sun through my dingy windshield and squinted. A tear of pain formed in my right eye. I closed my eyes tightly so it would touch my lower lid. I looked at the cop without blinking.

"You live in Burbank?" the cop said with a touch of sympathy.

"No," I said, "Pasadena." It didn't matter what I told him. If he looked at my identification carefully, I was in trouble. I beat him to it by pulling out my wallet and digging out one of the dozen business cards I had picked up in my travels. I handed him the card and he read it.

"Well, Mr. Dubliclay," he said, handing the card back, "I suggest you go back to Pasadena and have a nice quiet talk with your wife. She probably went straight back home last night."

Translated, this meant if you want to blow the head off your wife and best friend, get the hell out of Burbank to do it.

"Thanks, officer," I said, wondering if he would ever know how close he came to capturing public enemy number one.

I drove to Lola's apartment and made my way up the stairs without thinking about what I was going to tell her. No one answered my first knock. I tried again harder and Lola's voice said, "Just a second."

In just a second the door flew open and I found myself looking at Marco, who was pointing his hefty pistol at my chest.

"In," he grunted, motioning me in with his free hand. I stepped in, and he moved behind me to kick the door shut.

The room was small, hard and not inviting. The sofa and two chairs looked uncomfortable but durable, the way furnished-apartment furniture always looked. Sitting in one of the armchairs, Lola looked uncomfortable, too, but I couldn't vouch for her durability. She was curled up in a ball, one arm hugging her knees, the other one holding her hair back to look at me. She was wearing pink two-piece pajamas that made her look like what she wasn't, an innocent little girl. There was a fear in her eyes, too, that little girls only had when they woke up from nightmares.

When Marco prodded me with his gun, and said, "Have

a seat and . . ." I turned around with my elbow out to hit his gun hand. This time it didn't work. He backed up a step and drove his gun into my back. I staggered and Lola whimpered. I went into the wall, trying to make it look as if the blow had taken everything out of me and the crack of the wall had reduced me to bubble gum. I suppose if I had had time to think about it, I would have realized that the charade wasn't far from the actual feeling, but I told myself otherwise. Marco strode toward me, in command, hand cocked, ready to smash any disobedience that might be left in me. I kept my head down, watching with my eyes rolled up toward him. His blow wasn't as cautious as it should have been. I stepped inside it and the gun and threw a left into his stomach. The gun dropped to the floor, and Marco fell back on his behind. I wasn't sure how to attack a gorilla of a man who was sitting down on the floor. I couldn't jump on him or sit next to him. I could punch him while he sat, which would have worked out just fine, but some stupid nagging morality from old Gary Cooper movies stopped me.

My hesitation gave Marco a chance to recover. He went to his knees and dived at my legs. I started to back away, but he caught my left leg and I went over the sofa, landing at Lola's feet.

"Don't worry, I've got him now," I told her and got to my feet to beat Marco to the gun. It turned out to be a tie. In the next fifteen or twenty seconds we managed to prove once and for all that furniture in furnished apartments is not as durable as it should be. We went at it with more enthusiasm than the Underwriter's Laboratory could ever hope to get from a mere paid employee. I discovered that the leg of a walnut end table will not stop a charging thug. Marco, in turn, learned that a sofa pillow will not always hold up under the pressure needed to smother a detective. I was sure, as we thudded into the bookcase, that we would rate all the furniture very low for combat use.

We might still have been at the battle if Marco hadn't found himself at Lola's feet, following one of my better efforts at using my head as a battering ram.

"Don't be apprehensive," he told her and pushed his great body from the floor for another bruised charge at me.

"Hold it," I shouted, trying to catch my breath. I held out both hands to hold him. He hesitated. "Why did *you* tell her not to worry?"

"I'm protecting her," he said.

"From who?" said I.

"You," he said.

The fear in Lola's eyes was clear now. She was afraid of me, not Marco. I think I laughed. I know I groped my way to what was left of a chair. Marco picked up his gun and stood over me.

"What the hell made you think I wanted to hurt Lola?" I said.

"Mr. Lombardi said you maybe killed Larry and another guy and maybe you was planning to eradicate everyone in the Cooper movie, get them off Cooper's back."

"You thought I'd kill six or seven people just so Gary Cooper wouldn't have to make a movie?" I laughed. "Who would kill for anything as–"

"Lots of guys," said Marco, trying to button his shirt but unable to find the button I had chewed off. "I know guys have iced four, five other guys for less than five bills."

"Right," I said, thinking that Marco might be just such an icer. "But I told you I didn't kill your brother-in-law, Larry? I didn't even know his name and I don't kill people."

"I didn't like Larry much," Marco said, "but he was family and–"

"I know," I stopped him. "What's your wife going to say?"

"So?" he said.

"So Lombardi sent you to protect Lola from me?"

"You got it," he said, finally finding a button and a buttonhole, though they didn't quite match.

"Lola, you really thought . . . ?" I smiled sadly, but it was clear that Lola really did think it was possible.

"You ever stop to think that maybe Mr. Lombardi had another reason for sending you to guard Lola with this bull-fiddle story about me? Maybe he just wanted to keep you busy, take your mind off finding out who stitched Larry?"

"Mr. Lombardi wasn't culpable for Larry's getting his," Marco said, trying now to straighten his few strands of hair. We had broken the only mirror in the room, so he had to do it by feel. He managed to get two tufts up on the sides so that he looked like Porky the Devil. Then he pushed it back, but a crop of hair popped up in back, making him look like Tony Galento doing an imitation of Dagwood Bumstead. He was not a visually impressive mug, but he could throw a kidney punch with the best of them.

"Think about it," I said.

Marco's mind was not adapted to extended thought about much of anything. The idea of "thinking about it" seemed to cause him pain. He squinted to force the thought into action and gave it up.

"You're pulling a fast one," he said warningly.

"Suit yourself," I said. "Lola, you have broken my heart. I thought we were music together."

"Off-key," she said protectively. I couldn't tell if she was knocked-out drunk or shaky sober.

"Maybe," I said. "I'm not after you."

"Out," Marco ordered.

"No," Lola said hesitating. "I think he's telling the truth."

"You don't initiate no orders," Marco said in confusion. "I take my orders from Mr. Lombardi."

"This is my apartment," Lola rallied. "At least what's left of it after you two played cowboys and Indians. You want to protect me, do it in the hall or downstairs."

Marco was clearly confused. He couldn't shoot the person he was supposed to protect. He could shoot me, but even he saw that it would get him nowhere. I wondered if he was still afraid of Los Angeles.

"You still in love with California?" I asked.

He snarled, plunked his gun in his holster and looked at Lola. "You're making a singular mistake," he said, pointing a hot dog finger at her.

"That's my song," she sighed, finally letting her feet touch the floor. She looked tired. "Go tell Mr. Lombardi I appreciate his consideration. It's a real change from the memorable nights he tried to take me apart."

"You're making a mistake," Marco repeated, looking at me suspiciously.

"Hey," she said, standing on uncertain feet, "you've been a good fella. Don't make me call the cops."

Marco shrugged and went for the door. He stopped to think of another argument, but none came so he went out and slammed the door behind him.

"Well," I said to Lola.

She said, looking around the room, "Christ, this place is a mess."

"Sorry," I said, rising and moving around to see if any Toby parts were broken or severely cut. My body told me that I had escaped with less than I would have falling down a high staircase.

"I suppose I should pack up and move out before the landlord sees what happened and tries to make me pay." She picked up a lamp. It was a ceramic thing with a base shaped like a dragon. The dragon was now in two pieces. Lola held the two pieces, tried to fit them together, her mind on another planet.

I stepped forward and took the dragon halves from her, putting them down on the sofa. "Did you get any sleep?" I said, putting my arm around her.

"No," she answered quietly, chewing her upper lip. Her

eyelids sagged, and her voice was even more raspy than it had been before. She still held the smell of scented alcohol, and her hair filled my senses as she leaned into me. I wanted to cradle her, to look at her and try to sort out what I felt, what I wanted to protect. She was too wise and too innocent at the same time.

"I'll put you to bed and sit out here while you get some rest," I said, leading her to the only door in the room besides the one to the hall.

"You don't have to," she said, leaning into me as we walked, avoiding battle flotsam.

"I need a place to think," I said, supporting her through the door.

The bedroom was little more than a large closet. I eased her into the bed and onto the pillow. She kept her arm around my neck and looked into my eyes.

"You are a homely creature," she said, "but there's something in those eyes."

"Murine," I said.

"Don't wisecrack when the going gets serious," she said, pulling me closer. "You're a soft touch."

Maybe she was right. I gave her a friendly good morning kiss, expecting her to lie back and dream, but she turned the kiss into something serious, opened up and held on till I eased next to her.

"Well?" she said, wavering between a confidence she once had with men and a quiver that said I might reject her for something she had become. What she didn't know was that it was what she had become that brought me on the bed, not the tough girl that had started the whole thing.

Lola was warm and soft and tired. She was a wave, a soft wet wave and I floated on and in her. She was almost asleep when I finished but she managed a smile before she closed her eyes. I got up, covered her with a blue blanket and put my clothes on. Lola's snoring didn't bother me. In fact, I liked it. It was ironic. Lola had dreams of being a movie fantasy, a white-toothed, platinum creature with the sun behind her and Wolfgang Korngold music welling from the screen. She wanted to be a perfect fake. She was much more satisfying as an imperfect woman.

Since Lola was going to skip out on the apartment anyway, I didn't think there would be anything wrong in my making a few phone calls. My first call was to my brother at the Wilshire station. They put me right through to him.

"Toby, you asshole," he said, almost crushing his teeth. "Where are you?"

"Phil, let's talk sense and talk fast. You having Seidman trace this call?"

"What do you think?" he said.

"You're a cop," I answered, trying to straighten up the room as I cradled the phone on my shoulder. "I didn't kill that guy."

"Which one?" he said wearily.

"The second one, both of them," I said, looking around for a wastebasket and spotting a small one in the corner.

"I believe you," Phil said. "Now, what do you want? I'm a cop, not God. I can't say let's just forget the whole thing and go out for chop suey."

"Who was the guy?" I asked, trying to stretch the phone far enough for me to reach the wastebasket. I couldn't, so I tried pitching smaller pieces of garbage into it.

I knew Phil would talk just to keep me on the line to trace the call. I also knew it would take at least five minutes for a trace, and Phil and I both knew that I wouldn't be on long enough to allow that, but we had roles to play out.

"His name was Tom Tillman—small-timer, couple of arrests for extortion, one suspicion of murder," Phil said. "A local. You didn't know any of this?"

"No," I said honestly, trying not to cut myself on slivers of mirror.

"You think you might come in here and explain the whole thing to me," he said slowly, "so we can get working on it? The longer you stay out there, the worse it looks for you."

"You mean if I come in with my hands up, you promise me a fair trial?"

"Jerk," he hissed.

"And my old pal John Cawelti. You think he might get up a lynch party and rush the jail at night to string me up?"

"This isn't Tombstone," Phil shouted, finally losing what little temper he had left.

"Maybe it is," I said over his heavy breathing.

"Get your ass in here now," he shouted. I could imagine his face going to a purple-red like my father's used to do in his infrequent rages. It was a rage like that that finally made his heart say the hell with it. I always thought it was ironic that a gentle man like my father should lose his life in a moment of anger. Maybe anger needs practice. It couldn't just come once in a while. If that was true, Phil would live long.

"Phil . . ." I said, but he hung up. He had broken the rules. I considered calling him back. He had actually kept me on the phone for longer than I had planned, and I had almost forgotten the time. He wasn't supposed to get angry and hang up. I was supposed to do it with a flourish.

With a patient operator and a lot of time, I made seven phone calls.

First, I reached Carmen at Levy's and told her that I would pick her up at seven-thirty for the fights at the Hollywood Legion. I told her to come outside, where I'd pick her up. I didn't think Phil knew about me and Carmen. Actually, there was nothing to know. If they wanted me badly enough, the police would eventually make the connection, but by the time they did that, I'd either have some answers or be wrapped up and ready for delivery to them.

Then I called Lombardi, Mickey Fargo, Gelhorn and Bowie, accused the first three of killing Tom Tillman and Bowie of knowing more than he'd told me. I insisted that they meet me at the Hollywood Legion at staggered intervals of fifteen minutes, starting at eight. It was worth a shot. My last calls were to Jeremy Butler, Gunther Wherthman and Shelly Minck. I asked each to be at the Hollywood Legion, to stay out of sight and to watch for me. At a signal each was to step out and be a witness when I confronted the confessed killer. None had a gun, but I didn't think a killer would start blasting away in a crowded stadium.

There was no problem convincing Gunther. He simply said he would be there and asked no questions. Jeremy questioned the wisdom of the whole plan, reminding me of times in the past when my traps had turned into near-disasters for me.

"I know what I'm doing, Jeremy," I said.

"Yes," he agreed, "you are trying to get yourself killed. I'll be there."

Shelly was the toughest to convince. His excuses included: "Mildred wants me home to fix the oven"; "I have a sore toe"; and "My glasses are broken." The thrill of playing detective had faded with the first corpse, but Shelly rose to the occasion and finally agreed when I threatened to turn him in to the dental society for malpractice.

There was a lot of time, and Lola was snoring pleasantly in the next room. I cleaned up, found some Quaker Puffed Rice and coconut juice. There was no milk so I poured the coconut juice on the cereal. It tasted pretty good. I ate and read the few pages of Lola's newspaper that hadn't been chewed up by massive Marco and me. The Japanese had bombed an Australian naval base, someone had caught a four-ton shark and the Frankie Carbo jury was deadlocked. Carbo was on trial for the killing of Harry "Big Greenie" Greenberg. More important than all of this was the fact that

Sugar Ray Robinson had TKO'ed Maxie Berger in the second round of their fight in Madison Square Garden in New York. Somehow that reassured me that the world was still sane.

With a few hours to go, I looked in on Lola, who snored away. I found a razor in her bathroom, shaved and washed up. I looked presentable if I kept my jacket buttoned to hide the torn shirt.

I read a few pages of Lola's copy of *Saratoga Trunk,* didn't like it and turned on the radio. When Lola still wasn't up at six-thirty, I kissed her forehead and went out.

Carmen was as reliable as California rain. Al Pearce was just coming on when she stepped out of Levy's, her coat drawn around her shoulders. She looked big and strong and sure, even after a day of work; the reverse of Lola Farmer. I pulled up and got out of the car, looking around for cops, robbers, cowboys or Indians. The sun was dropping toward San Pedro when I opened the car door for Carmen.

"This will be a night to remember," I said.

"Oh, brother," sighed Carmen and off we went.

The Hollywood American Legion Stadium was as safe a place to meet a killer as possible. More than half a million people came there every year to see boxing and wrestling. Los Angeles fight fans knew that the best place to see movie stars is not on Hollywood Boulevard but in the first six rows of the stadium, which was one of the reasons Carmen got excited about going to the fights. She also had an honest respect for men who wanted to get rich by battering the other guys into submission or shame.

Eastern states, including New York, don't recognize championship fights held in California, where the state law limits all decision fights to ten rounds. But there is no lack of interest on the part of local fans. Henry Armstrong, ex-welterweight champ and former lightweight champ, lives in Los Angeles, but he never defended his title at home. Before

1915 boxing exhibitions up to twenty rounds were permitted in Los Angeles. I remember as a kid seeing a bloody one with Jack Johnson and a bald guy at Hazard's Pavilion at Fifth and Olive with my old man. Jim Jeffries fought his first pro fight in the old Manitou Club on Main Street.

Most of my own fights, including the one this afternoon, had come in or around Los Angeles, but no one had ever paid to see me punch and be punched. Maybe this would be the night when I got a chance to go one-on-one with a killer in the Hollywood Legion. Maybe the ghost of Jim Jeffries would be over my shoulder. Maybe I had the imagination of a ten-year-old and the brain of a flea. Then I found a free parking space on El Centro and waited in line with Carmen, who stayed close and looked around for celebrities. I plunked down a few bucks for tickets and we went in.

The wonderful trap of Toby Peters was set. Nick Charles, eat your heart out.

CHAPTER EIGHT

There were waves of olive drab and dark blue in the crowd, and the place was packed. Soldiers and sailors swelled the stadium, though the nonuniformed spectators still outnumbered them. The war made boxing even more popular. Maybe it was the fact that a boxing match has a definite start and distinct end, and there's a clear winner and loser. Violence, rules and no one gets killed. Boxing is war without the worst of war. I'd been at fights with servicemen before. There were two basic reactions. Before the fight they horsed around, spilled a little beer, argued about which was better–a fast-stepper or a slow, hard puncher. Then when the fight actually started, some of the boys went red-faced wild with every punch, their mouths open and moaning. Others sat back silent and serious, not knowing quite what it all meant to them, but knowing it meant a lot.

The crowd that night had the sound of fight crowds, a wave of sound pierced by an occasional loud, hysterical laugh or someone calling out to Maury or Al or Brian to bring back an extra hot dog or beer. Carmen craned her neck to see the ringside seats.

"I think I see Ann Sheridan," she said excitedly.

"Ann Sheridan don't come to no fights," said a bulldog man sitting next to her, without looking up from his program.

"I ought to know Ann Sheridan when I see her," Carmen insisted to the guy, who looked up from his program ready to fight and got his first look at Carmen, who was wearing her tightest red dress.

"Maybe Ann Sheridan changed her mind," the bulldog said with a twisted smile.

Carmen accepted his apology.

"Babe Ruth is supposed to be here," the bulldog said amiably.

"Toby knows Babe Ruth, don't you?" she said, taking my arm without stopping her survey of the crowd for celebrities.

"Sure," said the bulldog, eyeing me briefly and turning back to his program.

The hour hand on my watch was anchored now. It must have happened in the fight with Marco, but a firm grip on a small gear didn't mean a firm grip on time. I asked the bulldog what time it was, and a soldier on my left told me it was just before eight-thirty. A few minutes later the heavyweights in the first fight came down the aisle. The crowd cheered. The crowd booed. The crowd didn't know either one of the saps or their records, but they were big, and big guys gave out the hope of big punches. Both fighters looked scared. Both fighters looked young. One, a white kid with his hair cut short, was called Army John McCoy. The reason for the "Army" was made clear neither by the ring announcer nor our programs. The soldier next to me said he thought he was a soldier. Someone else corrected him behind us and said he knew he was a soldier. I doubted it but didn't care. The other fighter was a Negro kid with the biggest arms I'd ever seen and legs to match that might make him a little slow. His name wasn't even on the card, but the ring announcer introduced him as Archie "Black Lightning" Davis.

"I'll put up ten on Black Lightning," said the bulldog, looking around for a taker.

The soldier on my left dug into his pocket, and others rose to the challenge.

"Take the bet," urged Carmen, as the fighters in the ring got their instructions.

"The Army boy hasn't got a chance," I said. "The Negro's a ringer. I'll bet ten his name isn't Archie Davis. Look at those arms, scar tissue over the eyes. He's been around, and the other kid can't even look him in the eye."

I tried to spot Babe Ruth but couldn't. I sure as hell didn't see anyone who looked like Ann Sheridan.

For the first few minutes the two fighters received cheers for dancing. When McCoy decided that things weren't going too badly, he made a flat-footed rush and landed a right to Davis's head that Davis slipped. In return, Davis put a short hard left into McCoy's kidney that the crowd and the referee missed. The crowd went wild. It looked to them like McCoy had drawn first blood. The bulldog man looked over at me with a mean smile, and I nodded that I had seen what he had seen.

"Ten more says McCoy don't go the four rounds," the bulldog said.

Money came his way. Carmen dug into her purse, and I stopped her.

"He's right," I said.

I didn't have time to see the end of the fight. I told Carmen to enjoy herself, that I'd be back soon, and headed up the aisle before she could ask any questions. When I glanced back, the bulldog man was leaning in her direction, explaining the finer points of the fight game to her.

In the corridor the sounds of the crowd seemed artificial, like someone had created them for a John Garfield boxing movie.

The corridor wasn't quite empty. A woman rushed for the women's room. A guy at a hot-dog cart was counting his before-the-fights take. I spotted Gunther without any trouble. It is hard to miss a midget, especially when the midget is trying to look inconspicuous by standing against a wall reading a newspaper while a boxing match is going on that he supposedly spent money to see. Even the woman anxious for the toilet paused to look at him.

Gunther and I were at the right gate, and a wall clock told me that I was on time. A groan rose from the crowd, so I figured that Black Lightning had done his first evident damage. Curtis Bowie came loping along about thirty seconds later, looking a bit bewildered but holding onto his smile. He wore a dark ski sweater and a thin topcoat and had his hands in his pockets. I wasn't sure what might be in those pockets. I hadn't brought my trusty .38. I didn't expect a shoot-out, but you could never tell what a desperate human or a fool will do.

Bowie walked over to me and looked into my eyes, and the smile grew broader.

"I wasn't sure I'd recognize you," he said.

"Let's get down to business," I said. "Why did you do it?"

"The money," Bowie said, still grinning.

"Money?" I asked. "What money?"

"The money Max Gelhorn promised me," Bowie went on, scratching his stomach and turning his head at another echoing groan from the crowd. He spotted Gunther and was fascinated by the sight.

"Gelhorn paid you to do it?"

"Of course. Well, he didn't pay me but the guarantee was there," said Bowie, unable to take his eyes from Gunther and return them to me.

"So you killed Tillman and Larry from Chicago because Max Gelhorn paid you?"

"Killed?" said Bowie, forcing his attention from Gunther. "I didn't kill anybody. I was talking about the *High Midnight* script."

"If you didn't kill anybody, why did you come here tonight?" I said.

"Fargo killed him," said Bowie with a smile.

"Killed who?"

"Whoever got killed," explained Bowie. For a writer, he was having a hell of a time making things clear.

"Why?" I asked checking the clock. I had another possible appointment in a few minutes.

"A lot of hate in him," said Bowie confidentially, "and a lot of need. I can't see him being in the picture, but he'd do anything to get it off the ground, even more than I'd do. He'd kill for it. He said he'd kill to get this picture."

Gunther finally turned a page in the paper.

"You see that little guy?" asked Bowie, pointing to Gunther.

"Little guy?" I asked, looking around. "What little guy?"

Gunther packed up his newspaper and moved slowly away. Bowie shook his head in wonder, and the crowd roared again.

"Mickey would kill me, you or Cooper to get the picture done," Bowie said, watching Gunther walk slowly and reluctantly toward the men's room.

"You think he can reach the toilet?" Bowie asked.

"I wouldn't know," I said. The bell rang inside the stadium, and crowd sounds swelled. "Why would he want to kill Cooper? He's the goose with the golden face."

Bowie nodded and dropped his grin a bit.

"What happens if Copper gets killed?" he said.

"The picture deal is off," I tried.

The fight had obviously ended. People streamed out into the corridor, hurrying for the toilet and the hot-dog stand.

"Maybe not," said Bowie. "Maybe Mr. Gelhorn's backer lets Gelhorn go ahead with someone else. If someone kills Cooper, Fargo and Gelhorn aren't responsible for delivering him on the picture."

"You have a devious mind and a deceptive exterior," I said as a sailor jostled me.

"I'm a writer," explained Bowie proudly.

"How much did it cost you to get in here?" I said.

"Cheap seats, a buck," he said.

I pulled out a couple of bucks and said, "It's on Gary Cooper."

Bowie looked at the two bucks, was tempted, but plunged his hands deeper into his pockets to resist temptation.

"Nope," he said. "I like the fights, and maybe I'll pick up some material for a script."

Sometimes you make a mistake. My sometimes came more often than those of other people. I tried to restore some of the pride I had shot away by returning his status as a murder suspect.

"If Cooper got killed, the chances of your script being shot would go up," I said seriously. "Your motives might be the same as Mickey Fargo's."

Suspect Curtis Bowie straightened up and grinned at me. "Could be," he said and walked into the oncoming crowd.

Gunther hustled up to me and whispered while passersby watched us. "Shall I follow him?" said Gunther.

"Right," I said, resisting the urge to tell him to be inconspicuous. "Stay with him, and thanks, Gunther." Gunther disappeared into the crowd, and I went back to my seat.

Bulldog was counting his money and explaining the finer points of boxing to Carmen, who wasn't paying attention.

"You missed the knockout," Carmen said sadly. "Black Lightning electrocuted the army."

"Very colorful," chortled Bulldog.

"You get a jolt out of taking candy from soldiers who don't know the game," I said irritably.

Bulldog gave me a smirk and went back to counting his cash. There were guys like bulldog all over the stadium, guys who made their living knowing the fighters and the odds and playing on sentiment. Sometimes they lost, but usually they won.

In about three minutes the next preliminary bout was ready to go. Again one fighter was white and the other black, but this time they were welterweights, and both looked tough, and both looked like they were beyond maximum draft age. The white guy had a face even more mushed in than mine. The black guy had a double dark line under his right eye. The white guy had been around long enough to spot an old scar and work on it. If the black guy didn't nail him in the first round, the white guy would probably open the cut and work on it.

"I'm feeling sentimental," sighed the bulldog, talking over me at the soldier and then over his shoulder at anyone in the crowd who wanted to hear. "I take even money and take Monroe." Monroe was the white fighter.

The soldier next to me looked in his wallet and hesitated. He looked at me, and I shook my head no.

"I've got ten says Harkins goes for the knockout in the first. If he gets it, I win. If he misses, I'll go with the sentiment and take Monroe. I'm a sucker too," I said.

The bulldog leaned over and whispered to me, "Go work another area, you clown. This is my section."

When the fighters touched gloves, I whispered to the soldier to watch for a cut under Harkins's eye. If it opened a little, he should push for a bet and take Monroe. The soldier looked at my battered face, took me for an ex-pug and said thanks.

"I gotta go," I told Carmen. "Be right back."

"You have a kidney disease or something?" she said,

still looking for another glimpse of Ann Sheridan but also taking some interest in the fight.

Tall Mickey was waiting for me when I arrived at the stairwell. He was holding his coat open to reveal a jacket with buckskin trim, enough to suggest that he had something to do with horses. He looked even puffier than he had the day before, and he was worried.

Jeremy Butler was engaged in conversation with the hot-dog man. His eyes kept darting to me and Fargo, but he put up a good act. He wasn't as conspicuous as Gunther, but at six-four and almost three hundred pounds, he wasn't quite invisible either.

"Big bastard, isn't he?" remarked Fargo, nodding at Jeremy as I approached.

"Yeah," I agreed casually, "I think he used to be a pro wrestler. Can't remember his name."

"Talk," said Fargo, smoothing his mustache with a careful finger.

"You killed a man named Tom Tillman, a man you hired to force Cooper to make *High Midnight,*" I said smiling. "I've got proof."

"You got no proof," said Fargo, shaking his head.

"Then what are you doing here?" I said.

"I know who killed the Tillman character—the one who was trying to put the pressure on Cooper," said Fargo with an evil smile I recognized from moments on the screen just before Bob Steele wiped it from his face.

"Okay, who?"

"Gelhorn," said Fargo. "Son of a bitch probably hired the guy and wanted him to ambush you because you were getting in the way. Tillman fella probably objected, so Max and his temper took over."

"Gelhorn tell you that?"

"Max and I go way back," said Fargo. "Way back. I know how his mind works when the screws aren't too loose."

"And Cooper?" I said.

"What about him?" Fargo said, glancing again at Jeremy.

"Gelhorn's planning to get rid of Cooper," I said, looking directly into Fargo's eyes.

"What the hell for?" he said in surprise.

"Cooper's gone, and there's a new ball game," I said, taking Bowie's idea. "Gelhorn is off the hook if Cooper meets an accident. You don't have to deliver if your promised actor is dead."

Fargo touched his chin, and I realized that he looked a little like Pete, the fat evil wolf in Mickey Mouse cartoons. A thought had entered Fargo's fat head, and I had put it there.

"On the other hand . . ." I tried, but Fargo had had enough and pushed past me. He headed not for the stadium interior but for an exit. I nodded to Jeremy Butler, who returned the nod, disengaged himself from the hot-dog man and went after Fargo.

The fight was in the third round when I got back, and the black fighter's eye was pouring blood. He was trying to protect the eye, which reduced his offense to practically nothing. At the bell the referee called the doctor, and the doctor stopped the battle. A blood-spattered Monroe removed his mouthpiece to reveal a nearly toothless grin of triumph.

Bulldog leaned over to me and told me to keep my mouth shut or else. I laughed in his face. This time I talked to Carmen while the crowds rushed out for refreshment and excretion. The lack of kidney retention of the adult fightgoer is a phenomenon worth some study. I got Carmen and the soldier a beer and told them the main fight was a toss-up. The bulldog man, however, was not making the money he expected, and he was hawking it even for Morelia. I didn't stay while the ringside celebrities were introduced before the main event. This time Carmen grabbed my arm.

"Are you sick or something?" she said.

"Something," I said. "I'll explain later."

Shelly was at the hot-dog stand this time. He waved at me, and I pretended I hadn't seen him. He was chomping on a hot dog and had his collar turned up like Peter Lorre in a spy movie.

The corridor was empty this time. Everyone was inside for the main event.

Gelhorn's upper lip was pulled back as he advanced on me, showing even teeth that looked ready to bite. He wore a clean white shirt and carried his coat on his right arm. His right hand was covered and might be carrying something. I resisted the urge to move to the protection of the hot-dog stand. Not long ago on a case in Chicago, I had been shot while eating a hot dog.

"Well?" demanded Gelhorn. "What is this all about? And what is that fool doing over there looking at us?"

He pointed at Shelly, who turned his back.

"That is the man who said he was you," he said.

"Right," I said. "Let's get to it. You killed a man, maybe two."

"I direct scenes like this," said Gelhorn, looking to heaven for deliverance, "I don't fall for them. I didn't kill anybody." Gelhorn put his hands on his hips, cocked his head and looked at me with mock amusement.

"You need some dialogue rewrite," he said.

"I'll tell you," I went on. "If you don't deliver Cooper on *High Midnight,* some goons with guns are likely to come from the people who want the Cooper movie made and be really upset with you."

"Idiot," sighed Gelhorn, looking at his watch impatiently, his yellow-gray hair bobbing.

"Then what are you doing here?" I said.

"I was coming to the fights anyway," he said. "I like them."

"Sure," I returned, "five will get you ten that you can't tell me who won the first two on the card or who's in the main event. Why did you kill Tillman?"

Gelhorn took a step toward me. I didn't like the hand under the coat. A heavy figure lumbered out of the main hall, but I didn't look at him. My eyes were on Gelhorn's face, which looked more than a touch wild. I took a step back and glanced at my backup man Shelly. His back was turned.

"I met Mickey outside," Gelhorn said.

"Coincidence," I commented.

"Yes," said Gelhorn, "and he told me about your crazy idea about getting rid of Cooper."

"That's not my idea," I said.

"It's crazy," said Gelhorn, looking quite crazy enough to consider it.

"It wouldn't be much of an idea," I said. "It wouldn't work."

"No," agreed Gelhorn, without convincing me, "it wouldn't work."

I was sure I saw the glint of metal under the coat on Gelhorn's arm. Maybe it told me he was a killer. Maybe it told me nothing more than that he had brought a gun. His eyes told me that he might be wild enough to use it.

"You have any idea how much this picture means to me?" he said softly. "How long I've waited, planned? I've been in this town twenty-five years and never been offered anything better than second unit on *The Cowboy and The Lady*. I'm not going to miss this chance. Not you, not Cooper, not anybody is going to take it from me."

"Why did you kill Tillman?" I asked at the wrong moment.

"I didn't," he snarled, letting the gun come out a little further. He might have pulled the trigger. Maybe he was just putting on an act. I never found out. The burly figure that had come out of the stadium rammed into Gelhorn, sending coat and gun to the floor and Gelhorn staggering with his arms out to keep from falling.

"Hey, sorry," said Babe Ruth, clutching an armful of hot dogs and beer. Ruth winked at me and whispered, "Take care of yourself, Sherlock." Then Ruth rumbled off on his thin legs to find out what the crowd was roaring about. Gelhorn caught his balance and tried to regain his dignity. He moved for his coat, but I got to it before him and picked it and the gun up. It was a little gun. I quietly removed the bullets and handed it to him.

"The next time you point a gun at me," I said softly, "you eat it. Now I'm sorry if you don't like the line, but it's the best I can do."

Gelhorn turned and went. I looked at Shelly, whose back was still turned, and walked over to him. When I tapped his shoulder, he almost dropped his hot dog.

"I think he spotted me," Shelly said.

"You've been a big help," I said. "Do me a favor. Go to aisle 16 and find Carmen. Tell her my kidney gave out and drive her home."

"Mildred won't like that," he said.

"We won't tell Mildred," I promised. Shelly agreed and went into the arena.

Lombardi was scheduled to show in five minutes. He didn't. I waited ten minutes. Still no sausage mogol. In twenty minutes I gave up. I knew what I had to do. I had to find Cooper and warn him that he might be worth more on the slab than on the hoof.

I went for the exit, considering a call to my brother, but realizing that I'd have to do it on my own. At the gate a cop I knew spotted me and started to wave and smile. Then he remembered that there was a price on my head, and the smile faded. He started to stride toward me, with one hand going for his gun. I hurried through the turnstyle and ran down the street. I could hear his feet slapping after me.

My wind was good and the cop was overweight. He could have stopped to take a shot at me, but I didn't think he would. A lot of my survival lately was based on my judgment of human nature. If the past was any indication, I was living on borrowed time.

CHAPTER NINE

There was a character named Moneybags Farrell who ran a newsstand on Highland near Selma. He was called Moneybags not because he was rich but because he never handled his customers' money. He collected it in a leather bag. You dropped your money into it and he gave you change. Moneybags filled up the bag and took it into the restaurant on the corner every few hours. There he went to the washroom and washed the money before he handled it. Moneybags was convinced that money was the prime carrier of disease in the modern world. I told him once that others agreed with him, but he was the only one I knew who took it literally.

Because of his nickname, he had been held up twice by punks who thought he had sacks of gold salted away under *True Crime Tales.* Both times Moneybags had taken a slight beating and lost a few bucks.

I sat in my car with the motor running, listening to the Aldrich Family and reading the paper I had bought from Moneybags, who looked a little like my fantasy of Silas Marner from required grade-school reading.

I wasn't tired, and my mind was leaping with thoughts and fears. I considered heading for one of the hotels and checking in under a false name. I'd done it before and could probably get away with it again for one night, even though Phil would have guessed at the possibility. I didn't think the cops had the manpower to follow up on me that quickly. But I had work to do. I went to a phone booth and tracked down Cooper's mother. She answered after five rings. I reminded her that I had met her with her son at Don the Beachcomber's.

"I've got to reach him right away," I said. "Urgent business."

She made it clear that he didn't want to be found, that he wanted a few quiet days and needed the rest. I countered by saying I was sure he would want to hear what I had to say and that I'd take full responsibility. I wanted to add the words "life and death" but didn't.

Finally she agreed and gave me directions to an area on the coast in the hills just beyond Santa Barbara. It was clear that she was reading the directions.

"I thought he was going to Utah," I said.

She had no reply other than to tell me that she hoped what I was doing was really important. I thanked her, hung up and found a broken pencil in my pocket. I chewed away enough so I could scratch out the directions she had given me in my small notebook.

Ignoring the warning signs of my car, I got as far as Santa Barbara and decided to pull in at a rickety motel just outside of town. I'd stopped there before. They charged little, gave little and asked no questions. I told the scrawny guy at the desk to wake me at seven. He said they didn't wake people. I gave him a buck and he said he'd have the cleaning girl wake me. I gave him another two bucks to buy one of his shirts. He brought one out from his room behind the office and gave it to me without a question. I had the feeling that I could have asked him for his left arm and he would have given it without a whimper if the price was right.

There was no bath, just a shower stall, but the water was hot and the soap clean. The radio in the room didn't work, which was just as well. I slept and dreamed of Sergeant York picking off Nazis and turkeys. With each shot Cooper as York moistened the front sight and squinted before he shot. The Nazis turned into familiar faces–Lombardi, Costello, Marco, Tillman, Gelhorn, Fargo, Bowie and finally Lola and me. I tried to shout to Cooper that I was on his side, but he just lined up his sights, gobbled like a turkey and fired.

I woke up as the bullet sailed toward me in slow motion. I couldn't move, and I was sweating even though the room was underheated. Someone was knocking on the door and wearily saying, "It's seven. You in there?"

"I'm here. I'm up," I said, and up I got. The bed had been too soft, and my treacherous back ached slightly, but a second hot shower made it feel better. I overpaid the scrawny guy, who was still on duty but probably going off soon, for a razor and went back to my room, where I shaved while the maid began to clean up.

She was an undersized woman who looked like a walnut and sang something unintelligible and irritating, which hurried me through my shave and out of the room. Breakfast at a nearby roadside drive-in was corn flakes, sliced banana and a cup of coffee. I was back on the road by 7:40.

I felt a little sorry for the two figures in the blue Ford coupe who pulled onto the highway behind me. They had followed me from Los Angeles and probably slept in the car to be sure they didn't miss me. Maybe they had actually grabbed something to eat during the night, but maybe they hadn't taken a chance. In any case, I was in much better shape for losing them than they were for following me. Not only were they tired, *I* knew where I was going. At least I thought I did. I missed the turnoff a hundred yards beyond the Santa Fe Wines Billboard that Cooper's mother had told me about. I wouldn't have turned onto it anyway, but I would have liked the satisfaction of spotting it.

About ten miles further I came to a small town overlooking the ocean. I went down the main street slowly, with the Ford cautiously behind me. When I found a corner, I turned right and as soon as I was out of sight stepped on the gas and took another right turn. When I was back on the main street going toward the highway, I could see the Ford just making the first right around which I had disappeared.

Twenty minutes later I found the turnoff and drove down a narrow dirt road full of rocks. In about a mile the road gave out, and I pulled onto a grassy patch and parked. After locking the car and checking the directions in my notebook, I started up a narrow path through the trees. It was a great place to appreciate the outdoors, which I didn't. I don't like the rain. I don't like the sky over my head when I sleep. A nice, safe, enclosed room with artificial light and a steady temperature beats communing with bugs any night or day.

The shirt I bought from the motel clerk was a little tight, and by the time I wound my way up the hill, it was drenched with sweat. The cabin was right where Cooper's mother said it would be, a small, brick house built in the woods. It looked as if someone had designed it for a movie, right down to the pile of wood outside with an ax ready in a tree stump.

I went to the door and knocked. There was a shuffle inside and some voices before the question came, "Who is it?"

"Toby Peters," I said.

The wooden door unlatched and opened, and Cooper stood before me wearing a hunting jacket that looked like a cleaned-up version of the one Gable wore in *Red Dust*.

"What are you doing here?" Cooper said, stepping back to let me in.

"How about what are *you* doing here?" I countered. "You told me you were going to Utah."

Cooper shrugged and grinned sheepishly, "Just a little place I like to hide away in."

"If John Wilkes Booth had hidden here, he'd be alive today," I said, realizing that we were not alone.

The room was the room of men with furnishings most men couldn't afford. It was big, with a double bunk in one corner and a single bunk across the room. An Indian rug lay on the floor, colorful and new, and the redwood furniture with brown corduroy pillows helped the hearty-men image. A new oven stood in the corner next to a shining sink and refrigerator. If this was roughing it, I could take it. So, apparently, could the other two men in the room.

One of the men was a burly guy of about forty who stood over six feet and had the start of a gray-brown beard. He wore a lumberjack shirt and had a rifle cradled in his arms, aiming at the floor but ready to move on me. He stood next to the refrigerator as if guarding its contents from hungry intruders. The other guy in the room was dark and wiry, with a nasty scar that ran from the bridge of his nose, across his left eye and into his hairline. The scar was indented, and the man wearing it looked up without fear from the chair in which he sat.

"It's okay," said Cooper to the two men. "Mr. Peters works for me. That business I was telling you about with the Western."

The man with the rifle pushed away from the refrigerator and lowered the weapon. His face still showed distrust. The dark guy in the chair didn't move at all.

"Toby Peters, Ernest Hemingway and Louis Castelli," Cooper said by way of introduction.

"Luís Felípe Castelli," corrected the man in the chair.

Hemingway stepped forward and offered his right hand as he examined my face. He was interested in something he saw. I didn't outsqueeze him, but I held my own.

"Did some fighting, didn't you?" Hemingway said with interest.

"Not with gloves on," I said.

"I think I like him," Hemingway said with a friendly smile to Cooper.

I was hot and getting irritable and I didn't give a turkey's tassel what Hemingway thought of me. No one had asked me what I thought of Hemingway.

Cooper looked out the window and moved to one of the chairs, which he sat in slowly, cocking his head with his good ear in my direction.

"Hemingstein here," he said pointing a finger at Hemingway, "wanted to get away quietly. Buddy Da Silva is trying to get him to look over the screenplay of *For Whom the Bell Tolls,* and the Great White Hunter is not ready to make any decisions."

"So it's better to hide here than in Cuba?" I said, letting everyone know that I too knew who Hemingway was.

Cooper shrugged.

"Good hunting around here," he said. "Wild pigs. Some deer, even a cougar or two."

"Snakes," said Castelli with a distinct Spanish accent. "Rattlesnakes. Lots of them."

"Right," said Cooper, unperturbed.

"I've got reason to believe that one or more of the people on the *High Midnight* project might want to do you in," I said.

"Do me . . ." began Cooper.

"In," I repeated. "Shoot you, push you over a mountain or put one of my kitchen knives in your back."

He asked why and I explained; at least I explained everything but the possibility that I might be the one who planted the idea in the not terribly fertile minds of Fargo and Gelhorn. I also told him about the Ford coupe I had lost on the road.

Castelli leaped from his chair and went to the window with clenched teeth.

"The Fascisti," he said.

Hemingway went to the window and put his hand on Castelli's shoulder. "No, why would they follow Mr. Peepers?" he said.

"No, Mr. Heminghill," I said, looking around the room casually, "they just want to kill Gary Cooper."

Hemingway turned from the window, unsure of whether to smile or tear me off at the neck. "Your friend has a sense of humor," Hemingway said to Cooper.

"Every crowd should have at least one person with a sense of humor," I said over my shoulder.

"Meaning I don't," Hemingway said, moving toward me with clenched fists.

"I wouldn't know," I said. "I don't know you well enough, and I haven't read much of your work, but I've seen the movies."

"The movies of my work are crap," he growled.

"I like them," I said, "but what do I know?"

"Hold on," said Cooper, stepping between us. "Let's just figure out what to do while we have some lunch." Everyone agreed to that, and Castelli and Hemingway brought out bread, sliced chicken and beer.

"I think a man needs good hot mustard to tell him he's alive," said Hemingway, passing the mustard to me.

I turned it down. "Do you think you might tell me what's going on now?" I said to Cooper between bites and gulps.

"I've got to tell him," Cooper said to Hemingway. Both men had downed three sandwiches to my one. Castelli had been at about my pace. Hemingway agreed reluctantly.

"Luís here is in the country illegally," said Cooper. "He was a Loyalist, even though his family was nobility."

"I *am* a Loyalist," Castelli corrected. "The battle is not over. It is only delayed."

"Which," jumped in Hemingway, "may be why the

Spanish Fascists have tracked him across Europe and up South America. I got him out of Mexico one fart ahead of a trio of killers."

"They tried to split my head," Castelli said with a wild grin, "but they cannot kill me so easily."

"Glad to hear it," I said, to stay on his good side.

"The American government isn't exactly looking for Luís," Cooper explained, "but they aren't exactly welcoming him either. Franco says he's an international criminal and demands that he be found and sent back. Just to make sure, he's sent some people to try to get rid of him."

"And Tillman threatened to expose your part in this?" I said.

"Tillman?" asked Cooper, pausing in his consumption of sandwich to look puzzled.

"The number-two corpse in my room. The guy who looked like a brick."

"Right," Cooper said. "That, the business with Lola Farmer and a few other things that would not only embarrass me but my friends, particularly Hemingstein over here, who has committed a few indiscretions in his day."

Hemingway laughed, and the laugh made it clear that he and pal Coop were talking about wild sex and uncontrolled orgies, or at least hinting at them.

"The guy accused Coop of being a homosexual," Hemingway chuckled.

Cooper grinned and looked sheepish again.

I had fallen in with a den of boy scouts tittering about girls and bodily functions on their annual outing. I didn't laugh. Hemingway didn't seem to like the fact that I didn't laugh. He didn't mind that Castelli didn't laugh, but then again it was clear to all of us that the whack in the face that Castelli had sustained had done his brain no great good.

I finished my beer, and Hemingway finished his second or third. His hands were flat on the table, and he was considering something.

"What do you propose I do, Peters?" Cooper said, pursing his lips.

"I'm not sure," I admitted. "Probably stay here for a while, while I try to defuse the whole thing and find the killer. The police think I did it. I don't think you can stay here long, though. They might not be able to get the location from your mother, but one of you hunters must have left a trail here through a friend or a note or something. I'll stick around for a while to be sure the guys on the road don't double back and figure out where we are. I doubt it, but it might happen."

"Fair enough," agreed Cooper.

"How many of them are there?" Hemingway asked, touching his beard.

"Two," I said.

"There are four of us," he said. "Are we four grown men hiding from two guys?"

"I think it would be a good idea," I said. "They're after Coop, not the other way around."

"In the jungles of Africa, the countryside of Spain and China, I learned the hard way that the best way to keep from getting killed is to attack the animal, not give him a chance to go for you," Hemingway challenged.

"In the neighborhoods of Los Angeles, I learned that people with guns and knives and cars can hide anywhere and come at you when you least expect them," I answered. "It's the trouble with city living; the animals don't know the rules."

"Ever been in a war, Peters?" Hemingway said evenly.

"No, not the kind where they choose up sides," I said just as evenly.

"I almost lost a leg in Italy," said Hemingway. "Torn to pieces. I carried a man a mile with my leg mangled."

"I understand," I said. "You don't like to talk about it."

In a minute we would be one-upping each other with bullet wounds. I probably had Hemingway beat, but from the look of Castelli, he was the all-around winner. The man's face showed more defeat and dignity then any I'd ever seen. It was also touched with madness.

Castelli and I cleaned off the table while Cooper watched the windows, at my suggestion.

"How about a little exercise to get rid of some of this beer?" Hemingway said playfully.

"I can do without exercise today," I said.

"I've got a couple of pair of gloves with me," Hemingway said, looking at me with a clear challenge. "Luís doesn't fight, can't because of his head, and Coop can't throw a punch."

"Never had a fight in my life," Cooper admitted from the window. "Never learned to throw a punch. Still have trouble faking a reasonable-looking punch for a picture."

"My friend can't fight or play baseball," Hemingway said with mock pity. "But he can sure act. What do you say, Peepers? Just a little limbering up, no one gets hurt?"

I declined a few more times, and Hemingway upped the ante. In a few minutes he might actually slap me in the face with one of the gloves and give me his Authors' Guild card, if he had one. Hemingway was younger than I, heavier than I and probably a better boxer than I. He fished out some gloves and took his shirt off before putting on his pair. His chest was hairy and his shoulders broad. His stomach was a little fuller than he might have liked. Castelli pushed back the furniture and the rug and helped me put on the gloves. Hemingway got his on quickly and easily. Beware a man who carries his own boxing gloves and can put them on alone.

"That's a bullet wound," Hemingway said, staring at the scar on my stomach.

"One of those nonwars I was in," I said.

Cooper looked over at us and shrugged hopelessly in my direction to make it clear he didn't condone his buddy's idea of fun, but what could you do when an acknowledged genius wanted to play games. I marveled that Cooper could get all that into a little shrug, but that was his trade. Mine was staying alive.

Hemingway's arms were longer than mine, and he tapped me gently a few times. I pawed his hands away. Neither of us danced. Castelli stood to the side, leaning against the wall and watching silently. We went on doing nothing for a few minutes until I thought Hemingway had had enough.

"Let's call it a workout," I said, dropping my hands. Hemingway popped me in the face, not too hard, but not too friendly. If it was going to be the end, he was going to have the last whack, just as he probably insisted on having the last word. I threw a hard right at his stomach and came back with a left to his mouth. Blood welled around one of his upper teeth.

"That's enough," said Cooper, but Hemingway was happy now. This was real. This was earnest for Ernest. I let him hit me with a solid right to the side of the head, hoping it would satisfy him, but it didn't. He followed with a pair to my chest and a left to my head. The gloves were light and the punches hurt. I felt like reminding Hemingway that we were on the same side.

Hemingway had everything on his side, but I had a singular advantage. It was the one thing that probably made me a reasonable detective and a pain in the ass to have around. I just didn't give up. Hemingway continued to pop at my head, sending me back over the chair. I came up and went for him. For every five punches he gave me, I gave him one, but I was sure mine hurt. I went for the kidneys and the stomach. I got in a good rabbit punch when he ducked down.

"You crazy bastard," he said, unsure of whether to laugh or get angry. "There are rules to this game."

"This isn't a game," I said and went for him again. I thought I was Henry Armstrong. I probably looked like a bad imitation of an irate Donald Duck, but it was wearing Hemingway down. I doubted if he had ever been in a real use-what-you-can battle. Hell, I had been in one the day before. Pain was part of the job. For Hemingway, pain was something you learned to endure. You even enjoyed it. At least that's what he said in his books. I'd lied. I'd read more than one of them.

Hemingway began to pant and lower his guard.

"We'll call it a draw," he said.

"You call it what you like," I answered, putting the right glove between my legs to pull it off. "I call it a bunch of horseshit."

The rest of the afternoon was spent in silence, with each of us taking turns at the window. Eventually Hemingway began to ask me questions about being a private detective and a cop. He listened like no one I had ever met. His eyes told me that his mind was registering everything, and I had the uncomfortable feeling that I was being converted into a character for future use.

By dinner time we were so bored that we said the hell with watching the window for a few minutes and all pitched in to cook the roast Cooper had brought with him. Dinner was better than lunch, and Hemingway was mellow. We shared sad stories about former wives who misunderstood us, and were on the way to being besieged buddies. After dinner Cooper took apart and reassembled his rifle.

"Knows a hell of a lot about guns," Hemingway said, nodding at Cooper, "but not about how to shoot them."

"Maybe so," agreed Cooper, "but I'll outshoot you blindfolded."

Since I knew I couldn't shoot at all and had proven it as a cop and a detective, I let them rattle on and turned them off. They decided to test their abilities in an evening hunt. I suggested that they put it off till the morning to be sure I wasn't followed, but they would have no part of such cowardice. Out they went, rifles in hand. Castelli stayed behind, and I followed the pair further up the hill. The sun was setting but still had maybe an hour to go.

"Watch for rattlers," Cooper warned, taking long strides with his eyes on the ground.

I watched and followed them to the top of the hill, where they or someone had dug out a little pit to sit in. On the other side of the pit was a clearing for about seventy yards, and then woods.

Cooper settled in and pointed to the clearing.

"Water hole just beyond the trees," he whispered. "Pigs sometimes stick their snouts into the clearing."

"One hundred a pig," said Hemingway. Cooper agreed, and I checked my holster and .38, which could surely not kill a pig at fifty yards. We sat waiting with the mosquitoes and the calls of birds. Something that might have been a grunt sounded in the trees, and both Hemingway and Cooper sat up.

"How'll you know which one killed the pig?" I said.

"Dig out the bullet," Hemingway whispered. "Quiet."

Both men raised their rifles, and a miracle happened. The pigs shot first. A bullet dug up ground in front of the pit and a second one buzzed over our heads.

"Get down," I said, and both men ducked into the pit.

"They found us," said Cooper.

"Who?" said Hemingway. "The ones after you or the ones after Luís?"

"Got us nailed down," said Cooper through clenched teeth.

"We have the high ground," said Hemingway. "We can wait till dark and . . ."

"We have to get the hell out of here," I said. "It's as simple as that. We've got to get behind them, or they're going to keep us on this hill till they kill us. Do you have a phone in that cabin?"

"No," said Cooper.

"Is there some nice safe way down where someone can't hide and wait for us?" I asked.

"No," said Cooper.

"See my point?" I said. "One of you can stay up here and keep them busy. The other one can come with me and go around behind them."

"Right," agreed Cooper. "I couldn't make it down behind them without making a lot of noise, not with my back and hearing. I'll stay up here and keep them busy."

"I think I'd better stay here," said Hemingway. "My leg would slow you up."

I looked at both of them, and they looked back at me. Good-bye was in their eyes. It was my job and welcome to it, but there weren't going to be any words.

"Hell," said Cooper after a long pause and another bullet from the woods. "I'll go with you."

"No," I said, rolling over the side of the hill, away from the woods. Hasn't every private detective stalked killers in woods infested with wild pigs and rattlesnakes? This wasn't my jungle, but I was stuck with it.

The sun went down on one side of the hill and I went down the other. I got to the bottom before the sun. My feet had picked up about twenty pounds each and were taking on ounces fast as I made my way around the hill, trying to look for snakes and at the same time not be killed by hidden Fascists or some combination of Fargo, Gelhorn, Bowie and Lombardi, a firm with which I wanted no further business.

CHAPTER TEN

"What the hell are you doing this for?" I asked myself as I slid down the last few feet of hill drenched in sweat. I'm not sure I asked the question to myself. Hysteria was a real possibility, and I may have been talking aloud in spite of the potential danger, but it was a good question and one I couldn't answer.

I sat in a hole at the edge of the woods, panting. Nature had etched on me, using twigs, branches and rocks. A shot from the woods tore into the hills a few feet below the pit where Cooper and Hemingway were holding fort. One of them responded with a shot that came closer to hitting me than any enemy in the woods.

When I could breathe without making as much noise as the MGM lion, I ambled forward through the trees and bushes in a crouch with my trusty .38 in hand. When I hit a small murky clearing, a rifle bullet spat into a tree nearby and a voice shouted, "Stop there."

Part of the mystery was now settled. It wasn't a team of Fascists after Castelli. It was Max Gelhorn.

"Gelhorn," I shouted, "what the hell do you think you're doing?"

"You know damn well what we're doing," he answered. "We're going to shoot Gary Cooper."

"And me too?"

"Yes," shouted Gelhorn.

"And the two others with us?" I went on, trying to see where his voice was coming from.

Apparently he didn't know that there were four of us. I could hear him conferring with someone before he answered, "Yes. It's too late for anything else."

"I see," I said, moving behind a large rock and resting my pistol on it for support. "Since you've already killed, it doesn't matter how many more you do in."

"We haven't killed anybody," came Mickey Fargo's voice.

I could make out the two figures now behind a clump of bushes no more than forty yards away.

"It's kill or be killed," shouted Gelhorn. "Since I can't deliver Cooper and Lombardi insists on him, it's all I can do. You pointed that out."

I hoped our voices weren't carrying up the hill. My best tactic in case they were was to change the subject.

"Maybe we can nail Lombardi for the murders and get him off your back?" I said.

"No," cried Gelhorn, taking a shot in my general direction that came no closer to me than twenty yards. "Don't try to reason with me," Gelhorn screamed in anger. "This isn't a reasonable situation. This is a desperate situation."

To prove it a few more shots whistled in my general direction. Realizing that time was surely no longer on their side, Gelhorn and Fargo began to move forward in the bizarre belief that they were being hidden by shadows or trees or magic.

"Why not," I told myself and stepped out from behind the rock. Fargo was the first to spot me. He fired. The bullet hit about midway between us in the clearing.

"That's enough," I shouted with as much authority as I could muster. I raised my .38, aimed at Gelhorn's chest, knowing I'd be sick if I hit him, and fired. There was a scream and Tall Mickey Fargo, who had been standing five yards to Gelhorn's side, went down.

"I'm shot," he yelled. "Oooch. My leg. You crazy bastard. You shot me."

"You're lucky I decided not to shoot to kill," I lied. "The next one goes between your eyes, Gelhorn."

The two had obviously thought that their rifles were at a distinct advantage over my .38, but my fortunate shot had given them pause. The trick now was to keep from shooting again and let them know what a rotten shot I really was.

Gelhorn dived behind a tree, and Mickey hobbled to another one, still screaming ouch and calling me a crazy bastard.

"You're trying to kill me, and I'm a crazy bastard," I laughed.

"I'm shot," Fargo called back.

"That was the general idea," I said.

Gelhorn unleashed four shots, none of which put me in any danger. Mickey regained enough courage in spite of his knee to take a shot up the hill and one at me. His wound had improved his aim but not enough to make anyone worry. It would probably have been safe to charge right at them, but I wasn't prepared to take the chance, and I wasn't sure what I'd do when I got there. Would I really be able to shoot them if they didn't give up?

As the sun dropped over the hill, the problem was settled for me. At first I thought a wild pig had wandered into the battle. There was a sound like a squeal from the hilltop. My second thought was that we had awakened some historical ghost who was going berserk over our inept battle. A figure came over the hill a few yards from where Cooper and Hemingway were holed up. The figure came shouting down the hill with the sun blazing at its back. Held high in its right hand was the ax that had been imbedded in the log outside of the cabin.

"What the hell is that?" shrieked Gelhorn.

The madly charging figure was now close enough for me to see that it was Luís Felípe Castelli. He was shouting in rage as he charged toward the woods where Gelhorn was standing and Fargo kneeling, transfixed. Castelli was shouting in rapid semi-hysterical Spanish, and I could catch only a few words, one of which was certainly "Fascisti."

Gelhorn and Fargo both took shots at Castelli but probably came closer to shooting themselves than him. Gelhorn turned to run from this lunatic attack and almost dropped his rifle. Fargo yelped like a stepped-on dog and tried to hobble away as Castelli came crashing through the bushes and trees, swinging the ax.

I holstered my gun and tried to run to beat Castelli to the two terrified would-be killers, but my legs were heavy and tired.

"Luís," I shouted, "don't. They are not Fascists." But I might as well have been talking to a movie. Castelli continued the charge. I got to him as he leaped over a bush, landed in front of Mickey Fargo and raised the ax with a look of glee, ready to split the fat former cowboy into shank steaks. Fargo covered his head with his arms and moaned, "No." I caught Castelli around the waist and went down with him, rolling over.

"Luís," I said, trying to keep him from chopping my head off. "It's me, Toby Peters. *Cuidado. Basta. Por favor. No están Fascisti.*" He was a hell of a lot stronger than he looked, and if I didn't get through to him, I was sure he'd break away and start swinging, but apparently something I said or the sight of Tall Mickey convinced him.

"Está bien," he said softly. "It's okay."

I patted him on the shoulder and rolled away. Hemingway and Cooper were making their way down the hill, weapons at the ready. I lay there for about twenty seconds, catching my breath, while Luís rose and walked over to Fargo, who had thrown his gun away.

When Cooper and Hemingway stumbled into the clearing, I got to my knees.

"Mickey," said Cooper, recognizing the fallen figure clutching the wounded leg.

"Get him back to Los Angeles," I ordered, getting to my feet. "Call Lieutenant Pevsner in Homicide at the Wilshire district. Give him to Pevsner and Pevsner only, and tell Pevsner I'll bring in Tillman's killer by tomorrow."

"Who is it?" Cooper asked.

"Damned if I know," I said, slouching after Gelhorn.

"Always carry a lantern in the dark," Hemingway called cryptically.

Now what the hell is that supposed to mean? I asked myself without looking around as I stumbled into the darkness. At this point my clothes were so tattered that I must have looked like Rip Van Winkle, but I was unbowed. I could have stayed and tried to get some information out of Fargo, but he was more interested in his own pain than conversation, and it was likely he didn't know what I needed to find out.

I was weary, but Gelhorn was lost. Now I was lost, too, but I wasn't frightened and he was. A frightened man will make mistakes that can cost him his life. I lumbered after Gelhorn and in about five minutes heard him breathing hard ahead of me. Darkness had just about taken over, and I could have used a real flashlight instead of Hemingway's pithy metaphor.

"Be careful of the snakes," I called out. "Rattlesnakes."

"Snakes?" screeched Gelhorn and fired a shot in what he must have thought was the general direction of my voice. I plunged on, knowing that he was moving more cautiously now, watching the ground, which is probably what I should have been doing.

I almost tripped over Gelhorn when I found him leaning back against a tree, panting and looking downward, with his gun searching out rattlers in the dark. His curly hair was dangling in his eyes, and he seemed terrified.

"Give me the rifle," I said, leveling my pistol at him.

"Get me out of here," he pleaded, handing me the weapon. I took it and waved for him to follow me. I don't know what made him think I was any better at saving us from snakes than he was, but I figured I was no worse.

"First," I said, "you tell me everything about the *High Midnight* project."

"He'd kill me," said Gelhorn.

"I suppose that's possible," I agreed. "I'm not sure what I'd do in your place. Remember there's a lunatic behind us with an ax, and we're in a woods full of rattlesnakes. I'd say you have a more immediate problem than Lombardi. You're headed for a nice safe jail cell."

I couldn't see Gelhorn's face, but I could hear him trying to catch his breath. "Lombardi," he said. "Told me his part in it had to be kept quiet. He had two conditions. I had to get Cooper, and Lola Farmer had to be in the picture. It seemed like such a great idea. It was my chance. I took some of his money and developed the script, started seeing people, worked on publicity . . ."

"You spent a pile of Lombardi's money, and you found that you couldn't deliver Cooper and you couldn't give back the cash," I said.

Gelhorn brushed a bush of hair from his face and agreed.

"What else?" I urged him on.

"They told him to drop the idea," said Gelhorn.

"They?" I said, trying to locate Gelhorn's face.

"The mob, the mafia, whatever it is," squealed Gelhorn. "They didn't want the movie made, didn't want the publicity. They wanted Lombardi to keep a low profile. That was one of the conditions of letting him semi-retire to Los Angeles."

An animal moved in the trees nearby, and Gelhorn sobbed.

"Then why did he . . ."

"He told them it would be all right. I heard him on the phone. He told them not to worry, that he would keep his name out of it, that they should trust him."

"He wants to make movies and corned beef," I said.

"That's about it," said Gelhorn. "Now will you get me out of here?"

"Who killed Larry the Hood?"

"I don't know."

"And Tillman?"

"Tillman?"

"The guy who was hired to pressure Cooper, to blackmail Cooper, threaten Cooper into making *High Midnight,"* I explained, trying to ignore the animal sounds that were scaring me almost as much as they were Gelhorn.

"I hired him, but I didn't kill him."

I grabbed Gelhorn's arm and started to walk him in a direction I thought would get us out of the woods. I believed him, and that left me nowhere. When we got out of the real woods twenty minutes later, I was still in the woods about the two murders. We groped our way to my car and got in.

"My car's over there somewhere," Gelhorn said.

I threw his rifle in the back seat and told him he could send for it or pick it up when he got out of jail for attempted murder. Maybe pigs would wedge open the door and live in the car. Maybe birds would nest in it and rattlesnakes wend their way through the exhaust system. I didn't much care.

I put the Buick in gear, got stuck backing out, tried again and finally got the car turned around. We made it to the main road in twenty minutes, and I turned toward Los Angeles.

"I've never had a break," whimpered Gelhorn, pushing his bush of hair from his face. I glanced at him and saw that his cheek was splotched with dirt. He looked like a sulking kid whose mother wouldn't give him a dime for the Saturday matinee all the kids were going to.

"You don't just have breaks," I said. "You make them. Some people can make them. Others spend their lives sitting around waiting for them."

We didn't stop to sleep, though I did go to an all-night diner where they thought Gelhorn and I were escaped lunatics. We both looked it. I got down two egg sandwiches with mayonnaise in six bites. Gelhorn had a chocolate donut and a cup of coffee. He ate only half the donut. I ate the rest.

From that point on we said nothing. I didn't listen to the radio, and I didn't hum, whistle or sing. I tried to think, but I was down on my list of suspects. Lombardi was the logical choice at this point . . . or maybe Lola . . . or Bowie or—who the hell knew?

It was a little after three in the morning on Saturday when we pulled up to the Wilshire District Station and got out.

"Holy crap," bellowed the old desk sergeant, "what have you been wrestling, mountain lions?"

I didn't answer but pushed Gelhorn ahead of me toward the stairs. The old desk sergeant shouted at us to stop, but I kept on pushing, and Gelhorn stumbled forward up the stairs. The squad room was almost empty. The cleaning lady from a few days earlier was at it again, or still at it. She looked at us as if we were more garbage she had to take care of.

At his desk in the corner, Seidman was asleep with his feet up. I prodded Gelhorn toward him as the desk sergeant came running in, gun in hand.

"Hey you," he yelled, waking Seidman.

"I didn't think you ever slept," I said.

Seidman's eyes cleared immediately, and he put his legs

on the floor as he waved for the desk sergeant to be quiet. "It's all right, Bert," he said. "I'll take it."

Bert the desk sergeant put his gun away and went out, muttering and complaining about the lack of respect of the public for the police, though I could see no connection between the subject and what had happened.

"You're under arrest," Seidman said to me, rubbing his mouth and searching his drawers. He found what he was looking for: a toothbrush and a bottle of Teel tooth liquid.

"I've got answers coming," I said. "Soon."

Gelhorn found a desk and sat against it with his eyes down.

"When?" said Seidman quietly.

"Tomorrow; no later. Then I'll come in whether I've got something or not. You want me to promise on my mother's honor?"

Seidman smiled a terrible gaunt smile. "Who's that?" he asked.

"Name is Gelhorn, a movie director. He and an actor named Mickey Fargo just tried to kill Gary Cooper. Cooper is bringing Fargo in. I think," I said in a whisper, "you might want to ask them some questions about a hood named Lombardi."

Seidman was writing notes without haste.

"Cooper'll press charges against him and the other guy?" asked Seidman, getting up. His voice was down too to keep Gelhorn from hearing.

"I don't know. He'll probably bring Fargo in, but I don't know if he'll go for charges. Gelhorn and Fargo aren't going to try it again, not when you and the police department know about them. Besides, they were so bad at it that I'm not sure what they did would constitute a serious attempt. They're the ones who almost got killed."

"Tomorrow?" asked Seidman.

"Cross my heart and spit three times," I said.

"There's a coat on the rack near the door left by an

unknown client," said Seidman. "Why don't you take it and disappear? I'll wait till morning to tell Phil."

"Thanks," I said.

"You can get the gas chamber in this state for attempted murder," I said to Gelhorn as I passed him. "I'd tell them what they want to know about Lombardi."

The desk sergeant looked over at me as I came down the stairs in the coat several sizes too large for me. It did cover my ragged clothes. His face indicated a clear distaste for me and the direction of crime I probably represented.

I went home and to my room, checking to be sure that no prowl car was hovering in wait. And then I slept and it was the sleep of the just–deep, weary and undisturbed by dreams. My morning task would be simple: Find, confront and accuse Lombardi. If that didn't work, I could throw myself on the mercy of my brother and the district attorney, neither of whom was known to be particularly merciful.

Both the sun and Mrs. Plaut were in my room when I woke up. The sun was full of energy and pride, having broken through a week of stubborn, cold clouds. Mrs. Plaut's energy was no less determined. She stood on a wooden chair and was either adjusting or removing the portrait of Abraham Lincoln from my wall.

"What are you doing?" I asked. Fortunately she didn't hear me. As it was, she nearly toppled from the chair.

"What are you doing?" I shouted when she made it safely to the floor, portrait in hand. She heard that and turned to me with her lips in a straight, resolute line.

"I am removing the portrait of Uncle Ripley," she said. "I am also removing the bedspread and the doilies from the sofa. These are precious items for me, and it is not safe for them in this room, especially if you plan to continue to stab people and do who knows what else."

She scooped up the doilies and the bedspread. I was happy to see them go.

"And another thing," she said, marching to the door. "You will have to buy your own knives. Mr. Gunder," she said, using the name she had settled on for Gunther, "explained to me about those men being spies and you being a government exterminator. Frankly, as you know, I have always been a Republican."

With that statement of purpose Mrs. Plaut left the room with her recovered treasures, and I stood up to trudge to the bathroom, which was unoccupied, examine my scratches, take a shower and shave.

When I got back to my room, I made some five-minute Cream of Wheat and sat eating it with milk in the same chair recently occupied by two burly corpses.

I was pouring my second bowl when a knock came at the door. If it was the cops, I had nowhere to go in my underwear so I simply said "Come in" and went on eating. It was Gunther. The temperature was going up slowly, but Gunther was a cautious type. He entered wearing a suit, tie and vest, which probably meant he was going nowhere but had dressed for work.

"Toby, you are all right?" he said with real concern, eyeing the contusions.

"I'm fine, Gunther, just some scratches from a romp in the woods," I said and offered him some Cream of Wheat. He said it was after noon and he had already eaten lunch.

"I spent much of yesterday watching the man Bowie, whom I followed surreptitiously from the boxing arena," said Gunther. "He went to his home and remained there. I returned here last night."

"Thanks, Gunther," I said, tilting the bowl to get the last of the Cream of Wheat. "Anything else new?"

I got up and went to my closet. The remaining urban combat dress was sparse. I put on a pair of dingy dark trousers, a relatively clean white shirt I had been saving for an emergency, my shoulder holster and gun, a dark tie and a jacket I'd had since before my marriage to Ann. The jacket always made me think about Ann. She never wanted me to wear it, thought it was too long, out of style and ugly. It had been ripped up the back and sewn with the wrong color thread, which any human with reasonable interest could see.

"There is something else you should be informed of, Toby," added Gunther, sitting in the single soft chair. "Two policemen were here much of yesterday, according to the other residents. Mrs. Plaut welcomed them but seemed to have driven them to despair. They departed but said they would return this day."

"Thanks, Gunther," I said, adjusting my tie and turning around. "How do I look?"

Gunther was a good friend. He lied. "Quite passable," he smiled. "Another pair of pants might . . ."

"All I've got," I said.

"Quite passable," Gunther repeated.

Below us the doorbell rang.

"Maybe the two police officers," said Gunther, rising and hurrying to the door to open it. I stepped after him quickly.

The ringing went on, and that was followed by pounding at the door. The residents of Mrs. Plaut's knew better than to try to break through the sound barrier to her. We simply used our keys or gave up if the door was locked, which it seldom was.

"Anybody in there?" came a voice from below.

"That, I believe, is one of the police officers," said Gunther.

I recognized Cawelti's voice and nodded to Gunther as I stepped past him into the hall. We both heard the front door open. Cawelti whispered to someone with him. "If his car is here, maybe he was dumb enough to come back. Get up the stairs. I'll cover the back door."

I went to the bathroom in four soft steps and closed the

door most of the way so I could watch my room and the stairway. A burly cop I recognized trudged up the stairs, with his gun drawn, as quietly as he could. Gunther stepped back into my room. The cop didn't see him, but he moved cautiously to my door and stepped in. I got out of the bathroom and tiptoed to my room when I heard Gunther's voice.

"I simply have not seen him," said Gunther, spotting me over the shoulder of the cop as I waved and sidled past the open door.

"Are you some kind of German?" asked the policeman suspiciously.

"I am Swiss," said Gunther with real indignation.

Cawelti wasn't in sight when I got to the bottom of the stairs. He was probably waiting at the kitchen door to block my exit. I went through the front door and ran the half-block to my Buick. I was just pulling down the street when Cawelti came rushing around Mrs. Plaut's with gun in hand to see me. I made a quick turn over someone's lawn and sped down the street till I hit Fountain Avenue. I turned left, slowed down and then made a left on Western and drove to Melrose, where I made a left again and headed for downtown and my office.

I parked in back of a cleaning store on Ninth. The spot was reserved for the owner, but I knew the owner didn't have a car to drive. His name was Schoenberg, and I brought him what little cleaning I had. He had complained about being unable to get tires for his car and how he had to take the bus to work.

The rear fire door of the Farraday had no outside handle, but I knew Jeremy Butler kept it open when he worked, and since he worked almost every day, I assumed it would be open. Saturday was no day of rest for either the neighborhood bums or Jeremy Butler. I was right. On the way up the stairs, I spotted Jeremy on his knees, scrubbing away.

"I think it's tar or gum or some substance from hell," he

said, sitting and looking at me. He hesitated, put his brush down and looked at me from his scar-lidded eyes. "I lost that man Fargo Thursday. I'm sorry, Toby."

"It's all right, Jeremy," I said. "I found him. Any police around here?"

"That Cawelti, the one with the temper, was here," Jeremy said, looking at the spot on the stairs. "We didn't exchange conversation."

Jeremy and Cawelti had had a run-in a few months earlier when Cawelti had confronted me in the lobby of the Farraday. It was my considered opinion that Cawelti's life was a series of run-ins punctuated by violence.

"I'm going up to the office for a minute," I said. "If Cawelti shows up, try to let me know. If not, let's take a walk when I come down. I think I need more of your help."

Jeremy nodded and went back to the stair, his massive right arm bearing down with soap and suds.

My visit to the office was practical. I needed more bullets for my .38, and I had some in my desk drawer. I had used the gunful I had in my duel with Fargo and Gelhorn.

Shelly was working on a patient when I went through the door. He glanced over his shoulder at me, frowned and went back to the woman in the chair.

"I haven't been here, Shel," I said, stepping quickly to my office.

Shelly grunted, and the woman in the chair tapped her foot on the footrest in impatience or pain. I voted for pain.

"Mildred's angry," he said, and then he mumbled something like, "Where is that damned frubble-squeezer?"

"Sorry," I said, stepping back to the doorway.

"Mildred found out I drove Carmen home from the fights," he said, attacking the mouth of the woman in the chair with the frubble-squeezer. "She's jealous."

"I'll call her as soon as I've got things settled on the Cooper business," I said, reassuringly.

"She won't believe you," said Sheldon Minck, angrily

attacking his patient's mouth. The wretched woman whimpered.

"I know how to handle Mildred," I said, loading the gun. The patient in the chair was watching me through her suffering, and I couldn't tell if the fear in her eyes was resulting from seeing me load a gun or pain from Shelly's attack.

"You can't handle Mildred," he said. "She doesn't like you, doesn't believe a thing you say. She says you're a bad influence on me."

"She wants you to play with the other kids," I sympathized. "The ones from the right side of Figueroa."

"Something like that," Shelly said, going at the woman again, who groaned.

"What are you doing to her?" I asked with mild interest.

"Cleaning her teeth," said Shelly, pausing to wipe his sweating forehead and relight his dead cigar.

"How dirty are they?" I said.

"So-so," he countered, tossing the frubble-squeezer in the general direction of the sink and missing. The frubble-squeezer bounced onto the floor, and Shelly ignored it.

"We'll talk about it later, Shel," I said.

"Sure," said Shelly sullenly. I left and went down the stairs two or three at a time. Alice Palice of Artistic Books, Inc., was in the hall on the third floor, arguing with a couple of men in the shadows. They seemed angry. I hoped for their sakes they didn't get too angry.

Jeremy stood when I got to the step he was working on.

"These are good steps," he said, "but no creation of man can withstand man's own determination to destroy the artifacts of his culture. In Europe people still live in adequate houses built five hundred years ago. Here we marvel if a building stands seventy years. We are a wasteful society."

He gathered his pail and brush and walked with me down the stairs. We deposited the cleaning things in a janitor's closet and started out the front door. The street was crowded with Saturday-morning shoppers. Pulling into a space half a block away was a police car. Cawelti jumped out. Jeremy and I backed into the Farraday lobby before he could spot us. I nodded toward the rear and Jeremy followed me, moving more quickly and quietly than I did, though he outweighed me by almost a hundred pounds.

We went out the back door and through the alley. At the corner we turned right on Wilshire while I told Jeremy my plan and asked him to stay near his office phone. I might need some reliable help with little notice. He agreed, and I told him what I knew as we walked through Westlake Park. We sat for a few minutes under the eight-foot nude black-cement Prometheus, who held out his torch and globe.

"That was erected by Nina Saemundsson for the Federal Art Project in 1935," Jeremy said, looking up at the statue with admiration. "An underappreciated work. There is also a magnificent mural of Prometheus by José Orozco in Fray Hall at Pomona College in Claremont. It shows a huge Prometheus holding up the sky with small, gaunt people encouraging him."

I looked at the statue, pretending to share his admiration for Prometheus. My mind was on real bodies, not myths.

"The cost of bringing truth to men is often pain and eternal suffering," said Jeremy the poet, looking toward the playground in the distance. "I have a poem that might help you," he said, turning to me and putting a hand on my shoulder. "You want to hear it?"

I said sure. What else do you tell a 270-pound former wrestler with hairy arms thicker than radiators? He recited quietly:

> There is no end but death.
> We look for start, middles and end
> to give our lives a diameter
> controllable limits that send
> us a feeling of security,
> suggest an order

that is not there.
If there is a border,
we create it; and sense
is just a matter
of whose story sings
and whose song
you remember the melody of.

"Nice," I said, having, as always, understood none of it.

"It will be published in the Gregory Press 1943 edition of new poets," he said proudly.

"I'll look forward to it." I shook his hand and remembered when I did that in spite of his strength, his shake was firm and gentle. When you have the touch and are really confident of it, you don't have to prove it. I would have liked Hemingway to shake Jeremy's hand.

I stayed away from Hoover to be sure I didn't accidentally run into Cawelti on the prowl. Schoenberg let me use his phone to call Carmen at Levy's.

"Levy's," she answered.

"Carmen," I said weakly, "is that you, Carmen?"

"Toby," she said with anger touched with concern. "What's wrong?"

"Police after me," I panted. Schoenberg, who was a sagging man in his sixties with a sagging tailor's lip, stared at me over the pair of pants he was sewing. "Thursday at the fight I was kidnapped by Fascist spies. I'm working on a secret case. If I had gone back in the stadium for you, it might have involved you, and I couldn't do that."

"I thought you . . ." she began.

"No, never," I said. "I'll explain when I get this case wrapped up. Trust me. Got to hang up now. I hear them coming." I hung up.

"Take off that coat," said Schoenberg, "and I'll sew it good like new."

"No time," I said.

"It offends me esthetically as a tailor," he said with a heavy Yiddish accent. "I'll do it for free."

Five minutes later I was back in my Buick and headed for Santa Monica. The day was warmer, and the radio told me my time was running out. I'd promised Seidman that I'd turn myself in, killer or no killer, sometime today. Officially, today ran till midnight. I took Santa Monica Boulevard, Route 66, and tried to think out my dialogue with Lombardi.

Ann, the former Mrs. Toby Peters, had once said that my greatest drawback was my inability to plan ahead, even when not doing so might be dangerous to life and limb. While I had to agree with Ann that it was a shortcoming, I couldn't rank it at the top. To give her credit, she was constantly changing the item to top the list of the major drawbacks of life with Toby Peters. Just before she walked out for the first, last and only time, we agreed that the list of my faults, if published, would rival the Greater Los Angeles telephone directory in volume.

So I headed for a confrontation with Lombardi in the hope that the right words would come when the time came. It was my style, and I accepted it. It was a simple plan which had seen me through life but done my body no great good. Step one, plunge yourself in and make your opponent angry. Step two, provoke him or her a little more. Step three, hope they respond to prove you were right. (Parenthetical remark to step three: hope you survive the attack.) Step four, set up a trap so you nail them. I knew there were smarter ways to work, but a man gets into habits and learns to live with them and even savor them. This was the patented Toby Peters method. I could open a school and teach it: a half-day course in being a private detective.

I remembered a line from Jeremy's poem and asked myself, "Whose song do you remember the melody of?" The music to "Over There" popped into my head. It was my father's favorite song, along with "The Bird in the Gilded Cage." I sang them both on the way to Lombardi's and finished when I pulled into the now-familiar parking lot.

CHAPTER ELEVEN

An overnight rain had turned the parking lot into Mudville. I walked carefully around piles of bricks and puddles. There were no construction workers hammering or mortaring merrily away. It was Saturday. It was also possible that my number-one suspect, Lombardi, might not be at the factory, but I had no place else to try, and time was running out.

The rear door was open, and I stepped into darkness.

"Hey," I called, not wanting to get an accidental blast in the stomach from a jumpy watchman. "Anybody here?"

My eyes got used to the darkness, and I sidestepped machinery and boxes and found my way forward by the scent of garlic.

"Anybody here?" I tried again, running my hand along the wall I had found and going for the door I remembered. I found it and opened it to find myself facing the two sausage workers in white. The kosher one, Steve, was pointing a gun at my chest.

"You are trespassing," he said evenly. The other guy kept his hands in his pockets. "I wonder what Mr. Lombardi will want us to do with this trespasser?"

"Mr. Lombardi will want to talk to this trespasser," I

said. "I've got information for him that he wants. He's expecting me. Just tell him it's what I was going to give him on Thursday."

Steve looked at his co-worker, chewed on the inside of his right cheek pensively and nodded toward a door in the far corner of the storefront. This was a room bright with light from the windows. Outside, a passerby looked through the window, curious about the new store in the neighborhood.

"Thanks," I said.

"We'll be waiting right here," Steve said. "We'll see what Mr. Lombardi decides to do with you."

The threat of my own kosher future hovered in the air with the smell of garlic and spices as I walked to the door and reached for the handle.

"Hold it," shouted Steve, running up to my side. I held it.

Steve patted me down and found the .38. He pulled it out and gave me a dirty look.

"You almost let me get by with that," I said with a shake of my head, to indicate that he might be losing his touch. "I won't mention it to Mr. Lombardi."

"You'll get it back on the way out," he said. "If you go out."

I knocked on the door as Steve stood back to stand guard and wait for the roar of Lombardi that would end my brief passage on earth in human form. Lombardi said nothing, so I stepped in, closed the door behind me and counted on whatever gods there might be to provide me with the right words.

Lombardi had his back turned, and I started to talk.

"Before you do something you and I will regret," I said, "let me talk. I've told someone I'm coming here. If anything happens to me, he'll tell the police. I'm supposed to give him a call every fifteen minutes. I don't want any trouble. I just want to straighten things between me and the police."

Lombardi said nothing and didn't turn around. There was something in the atmosphere of the room, something I recognized from experience. It was the silence of death, and since I was still alive and Lombardi wasn't moving, I placed my bet on him. I went around the desk and found out I was right.

This time the knife was in his chest. Lombardi looked surprised, skewered in his own sausage factory, his plan of corned-beef conquest ended before it really began.

With the departure of Lombardi's soul, if there were such a thing, went the last clear suspect on my list. I was back at the start–well, almost at the start. Lombardi was now off my list of suspects. Most victims have that as doubtful consolation.

"Everything all right, Mr. Lombardi?" asked Steve outside the door. I could see his shadow on the glass.

"It's okay," I said, holding my hand over my mouth. I tried to put some anger in the words, but I didn't want to use enough words to make him doubt the voice.

"I'll be right out here," said Steve.

I grunted and went on, talking in my own voice.

"Okay, so we understand each other. You've got my word that I'll never bother you again, and you agree to let me step out of this with my own skin instead of the one you put on the hot dogs. I appreciate your understanding, and you can count on me."

My choices were few. I could call Steve in and show him Lombardi's corpse. There was an outside chance he would believe I hadn't just walked in and played Zorro. But even if he believed me, there was a chance he might not let me go. I had no gun and could find none on Lombardi's corpse or in his desk.

Lombardi's white smock was stained with red now, and he looked like a butcher who had been turned against by one of the steers ready for slaughter. There was no blood on me as I went to the door, saying "Thanks" to the corpse as I backed out and shut the door.

Steve faced me and looked at the office door.

"Mr. Lombardi says he doesn't want to be disturbed," I said, putting out my hand for the gun.

Steve hesitated, looked over at his co-worker and handed me my .38.

"Mr. Lombardi is a very understanding man," I said, going to the front door and turning the handle. The door was locked. I tried not to show panic as I walked past Steve and headed for the door leading to the dark room beyond and the parking lot and the relative safety of my car beyond that.

I was almost touching the door when it opened and Marco stepped in.

"What's going on?" he demanded, looking at me. "I go out five minutes and this mug is on the premises. You can't see Mr. Lombardi. He don't want to see you."

"I just saw him," I said. "We've got everything straightened out."

Marco cocked his big bald head and looked at Lombardi's door.

"I want to hear him say that," he said.

"It's true," said Steve, backing me up with what he thought he had heard. "Mr. Lombardi doesn't want to be bothered now."

Marco looked back at me suspiciously as I walked slowly through the door. Once in the dark, panic came, and I rushed toward the spot of light on the far wall that marked the exit. I cracked my knee on something short and hard and hobbled forward without making a noise. The Buick was at least six hundred yards away in the parking lot. Well, maybe it was twenty yards away. I was carrying the ball through mud, knowing the tacklers were not far behind.

The car stalled in the mud and the wheels spun. I took a deep breath, counted to five, took my .38 out and put it at my side, watching the door while I tried again slowly. This time the car moved backward, and I let it have its own head till I felt the wheels touch something solid. Then I tore forward over rubble, leaving the lot and the factory behind.

As I drove, I mused over whether by nightfall there would be any organized group in the Greater Los Angeles area that would not be trying to find me. I wasn't sure who I'd prefer to take my chances with, Cawelti or Marco and company. The only one I could think of who might frighten both of them was Luís Felípe Castelli, but he had his Fascists, assumed and real, to deal with. My battle was on a less global scale but no less important to me.

My stomach grumbled with hunger. I told my stomach it was just doing that because I was confused and scared. It always tries to distract me when things go wrong, but there is no reasoning with an insistent stomach. I fed it some burgers and a Pepsi and then cursed it for its impatience when I spotted a taco stand a block further on. I stopped for the taco anyway, and my stomach got quiet. Then the Buick began to complain and with good reason. It was out of gas. I coasted for half a block to a Texaco station and pushed the car the rest of the way to the pump.

Next stop: the Big Bear Bar in Burbank. The front door was open, but there was no sound from inside. This time I just stood inside the door while my eyes adjusted. Nothing stirred. In a few seconds I could see Lola across the room sitting at the piano, staring at nothing and not playing. For a second she looked like the girl in *White Zombie,* but the smell of death wasn't in the room.

"Lola," I said quietly.

She turned around and looked at me. Something like a smile touched the corner of her mouth. She automatically reached for a drink on the piano, but it wasn't there, so she shrugged instead and started playing "In the Good Old Summertime."

"Lola," I said again, and she stopped.

"You have bad news," she said. "I can spot the bringer of bad news two blocks away. I know a guy who has been known to knock off bringers of bad news."

"Just like the Greeks I remember reading about in high school," I said.

"He is no Greek," said Lola with a small, sad laugh.

"You talking about Lombardi?" I said, walking through the tables.

"None but," she said, fingers poised over the keys.

I sat down and put my arm around her. She sagged next to me.

"Lombardi is dead," I said. I could feel her shudder, and I didn't like myself. I hadn't told myself what I was doing, but I knew. I had been testing Lola, had held her to see her reaction, to judge if she might have punctured Lombardi or if she knew about it. I would have bet she didn't, but then again she was an actress.

"Dead?"

"Dead," I repeated.

"That's the end of Lola's comeback," she said, hitting one key and sending the echo of its music through the darkness. "That was a selfish thing to say, but it's what I was thinking."

"Then you might as well say it," I said, cradling her head. "Can you answer some questions for me?"

She didn't speak, just leaned against me, dreaming of the movies that would never be.

"Lombardi put up the money for *High Midnight,*" I said. "Why?"

"He said he owed it to me," she answered dreamily. "But you know what I think? I think he just wanted an excuse to put the screws on Cooper to even things up. Lombardi and I were through a long time ago, but he hated Cooper for the few days I spent with him almost, hell, eight or nine years ago. He didn't forget all that time. Lombardi is . . . was . . . the kind that wanted the score at least even, even if the game didn't matter anymore. He thought it was a sign of weakness if you left a situation with the other guy up on you.

"The boys back East told him to forget it," she went on. "They said it nice at first and then they said 'or else,' but old Chuckles Lombardi wouldn't let go."

"So you think somebody back East ordered Lombardi killed?"

"Who knows?" she said, pulling away from me and heading for the bar. "I'd say our dear departed Mr. Lombardi left a trail of enemies from Naples to Frisco."

Lola went behind the bar and mixed herself something while I sat in silence, and the minutes ticked away. I started to play chopsticks, and Lola, drink in hand behind the bar, laughed. It wasn't a pleasant laugh. She hustled back to the piano, sat at my side and joined me. We played seriously, sour, missing notes, and sat still when we finished the only piece I knew.

"And now?" I said.

She was wearing a yellow dress made of some silky material. The dress matched the color of her hair, at least in the darkness.

"The Big Bear Bar in Burbank," she said, taking a drink. "That's the end of the road for Lola Farmer. Can I confess something to you?"

"My pleasure," I said.

"My name is not really Lola Farmer," she said in a confidential whisper. "I used the name Farmer because my father was a farmer. My name is Betty Davis. I swear, Betty Davis. Now there just isn't room in Hollywood for two Betty Davises, so I decided nobly when I was a kid to back away and choose another name. You know who picked the name Lola Farmer? Lombardi."

"Lola, I'll be back when I get some things settled," I said, getting up and touching her shoulder. She shrugged, and I went on, "I've got to turn myself in to the cops. Maybe they'll figure out who carved up Santucci, Tillman and Lombardi. I sure as hell can't."

She waved at me without looking up and started to play and sing the saddest version of "Happy Days Are Here Again" that a human could create. Off-key and all, I liked it.

On Buena Vista I found a phone booth and gave the operator the number while I watched the sun start to go down. It was still afternoon and there was still time for a miracle, but I wasn't counting on one. I called my office and let the phone ring about fourteen times before Shelly answered.

"Sheldon Minck, oral surgeon," he said.

"You are not an oral surgeon," I said. "You are a dentist. You can go to jail twenty years for saying you're an oral surgeon. How the hell do you know who's going to call you and hear you say that?"

"I don't tell you how to be a detective so you . . ." then he remembered the masquerade of his which had started the whole thing. "Maybe you're right," he said sullenly.

"Any calls, Shel?" I asked.

"Maybe I could become a real surgeon," he said. "I know a place in Ventura that will give me a degree for $40. That's pretty steep, but . . ."

"Shelly, any calls?"

"Yeah, just a minute." He dropped the phone and wandered off in search of the message. I could hear cups, metal and paper being moved in a search for the message. In about three minutes he came back and said, "Here it is. A number. You're supposed to call right away. Urgent."

"Who is it?" I said, taking the number he gave me.

"Hayena, or something like that," said Shelly. "Say, will you call Mildred tonight and explain to her about Carmen? I don't think I can go home and face that."

"I'll probably be in jail tonight, charged with murder," I said. "Three murders."

"They let you have a phone call," Shelly said. "You can call Mildred."

"I'll think about it, Sheldon," I said, hanging up. I answered the urgent message from the man named Hayena.

This time the phone was picked up after one ring. "Yeah?" came the voice.

"Toby Peters," I said. "I'm returning your call."

"I gotta talk to you, Peters," he said. I recognized the voice. It was Marco.

"Your name is Hayena?" I asked.

"Hanohyez," he said impatiently, "Marco Hanohyez."

"I never knew your last name," I said quietly.

"Well, now we been introduced formally," he said. "Let's get together."

"I didn't ice Lombardi," I said.

"I know," he answered. "I think I know who did. Can you rendezvous with me? I want to get this over with and get back to Chicago. I think I felt an earth tremor today."

"Why don't you just tell the cops who killed Lombardi?" I said suspiciously.

"Sure," he said with reasonable sarcasm. "The cops'll listen to me."

"How do I know you're not setting me up because you think I knifed Lombardi?"

"Suit yourself," he said.

What did I have to lose besides my carcass?

"Where do you want to meet?" I said.

"That Coney Island place," he said. "I don't know my way around, but I am capable of getting there from here."

"Ocean Park," I said. "I'll meet you on the walk outside the entrance of the Dome Pier. In an hour."

"Hell, no," said Hanohyez. I preferred him as Massive Marco, but truth has a way of shoving itself in your face and making your life more difficult. "I can't get away from these guys now. Lombardi's crew is having a council. They're all discombobulated. I just . . . they're calling me back. Midnight at that Dome Pier place."

"Wait . . ." I said but he had hung up.

Midnight was my deadline for turning myself in to Seidman. If I had anything to sell in my profession it was my silence and my word, but I knew I would have to meet Hanohyez. I knew it was the one thing that might end this whole case.

I called Jeremy Butler with a message and got in my car. I had some time to kill, so I drove to Griffith Park and looked at the chimps. Looking at the chimps always calmed me down. I needed calming down. Then, suddenly, everything made sense. It was a wacky kind of sense, but it was sense. I was listening to my own song. The chimp laughed at me, and I grinned back at him. My grin frightened him and he rolled back into a corner to suck his thumb.

CHAPTER TWELVE

In 1892 the Santa Fe and Santa Monica Railroad finished a line from Los Angeles to Ocean Park, which was then known as South Santa Monica. The railroad built a station, an amusement pavilion and cement walkways along the beach. Excursions were advertised to the "Coney Island of the Pacific." It worked, and golf courses and racetracks followed. Between 1909 and 1916, Santa Monica was regularly drawing thousands for the Santa Monica automobile road races.

In the 1920s, lured by sea breezes and commuter trains, movie stars, writers, directors and moguls built summer houses on the beach. The resort image faded a little in the 1930s and 1940s and moved to Venice, Redondo and down the coast, but Santa Monica wouldn't give up its nickel-and-dime weekend trade. The big industry, however, was the Douglas Aircraft Company, which got to be an even bigger industry when the war began.

In 1942 Ocean Park couldn't make up its mind what to be or do. The war and invasion fear, which led to blackouts, kept the place operating mostly during the days. Decay threatened to set in, but the arcade and ride owners still found it profitable to keep up with repairs and wait for the next boom.

It was a little before midnight when I turned right off of Fourth and went down Ashland Avenue toward the ocean. I parked in front of the Municipal Auditorium and got out. A night gull soared over the concrete plaza and dive-bombed the bandshell. I didn't see anybody. I headed toward the walkway, running along the Dome Pier, but I didn't get more than a dozen feet when the voice came out of the darkness near a stucco-covered pillar.

"Peters, here."

I looked "here" and saw Hanohyez step out of the shadow. At least it was the shape of Hanohyez. It was difficult to think of him as anything but Massive Marco, but my mind was working hard at it and other things.

"I thought we were supposed to meet on the edge of the pier?" I said aloud.

He stepped toward me, motioning me to be quiet. When he got to my side, he looked around and whispered, "Let's keep this quiet." He hunched his shoulders up like James Cagney and looked around. "I don't know if them guys followed me. I don't think so, but I reconnoitered. Why chance it, you know?"

He guided me into the shadows and toward the shoreline, walking away from the pier.

"I want to show you something," he said, leading the way. We moved quickly past a hot-dog stand and some game stands, all closed, that urged people to knock Negroes off perches, slam baseballs into dolls that looked Oriental and throw darts at cartoons of Hitler.

"Will you look at that?" Hanohyez marveled, pointing at his discovery. "A little tiny golf course."

We were standing in front of a pee-wee golf course, and Hanohyez was displaying it to me proudly. "I never played the game," he said, "but I accompanied the big guy once when he played."

"Big guy?" I said.

"Capone," he answered, looking over the course and looking back at me.

"It's nice," I said.

"The things they think of," Hanohyez said, walking reluctantly from the little golf course.

"There's a fun house over there," I said, trying to lead him in the opposite direction.

"Let's talk," he said, pausing on the cement promenade and looking out at the ocean for incoming enemy subs. Far down the walk a figure moved slowly. We both kept our eyes on it till it turned inland and disappeared.

"Okay," I said. "You think you know who killed Lombardi, Tillman and your brother-in-law Larry."

"I know," he said, taking a deep breath of air. All I could smell was the dead fish. "That was a sharp trick this afternoon, smart trick. Real prestidigitation. Had those guys fooled. You really did an act, like . . . like Bogart or one of those guys."

"Thanks," I said. "The killer?"

But Hanohyez wanted to engage in a little more admiration of my masquerade. "I coulda swore Lombardi was extent in there," he said. "Steve did swear it, but I knew he wasn't." A cool breeze brought a fresh burst of fish odor.

"You knew he wasn't alive?" I said with interest.

"Sure, I'd killed him more than an hour before," he said, without turning to me. "You think that roller coaster is bigger than the Bobs at Riverview?"

"Riverview?" I said, looking for the closest building and wondering if I could get to my gun.

"In Chicago," Hanohyez said.

"I wouldn't know," I replied, trying to inch my hand up to my chest and making it look like a casual gesture.

"You helped me," he said. "I mean you facilitated things for me. Thanks."

"Glad to do you a favor," I said.

My hand was almost at the Napoleon position when Hanohyez withdrew his right mitt filled with a .45. He pointed at my chest. I took my hand out of my coat, and he reached in carefully and took my .38.

As he put it in his pocket, he looked around to be sure we had no company. The mad gull or his cousin came screaming over us.

"We got no birds like that in Chicago," he said. "It is not an aviarian city." And then back to business. "Steve and Al and me all found Lombardi together when you went out. Since he was living when you walked in, or so they thought, and dead when you went out . . ."

"I must have killed him," I concluded. Hanohyez nodded.

"That won't hold up," I said.

"Maybe, maybe not," he shrugged. "It'll be good enough with Lombardi's boys, specially if you ain't around to contradict any other way. Then I can get out of here before the Jap attack. Hell, they'll even thank me for doing you."

"You'll get the pickled tongue of honor," I said.

"I never thought you was risible," he said, holding the gun up to my chest.

"You came to Los Angeles to kill Lombardi," I said.

"Right, me and Larry came because some guys thought Lombardi was making embarrassing noises about making movies and being a big man, and he wouldn't listen rational. Some guys in New York asked some guys in Chicago to send someone who knew his stuff to Los Angeles to zip Lombardi's mouth."

"And he thought you came out to help him start his deli supply boom?"

"On the nose. You got two more queries and quick ones before you expire."

"You killed Tillman?"

"Tillman?"

"The guy in my room," I explained.

Hanohyez looked over his shoulder to check again on possible company. He wasn't going to let this go on long, and I couldn't see a hopeful direction to jump.

"He killed Larry," Hanohyez explained. "I was surveillancing your place for you to come back when I saw him going in. I think he was going to work you over or rub you out. My killing him saved you from something."

"Thanks," I said.

He nodded. "He turned on Larry outside that bar in Burbank where we tailed you. When I came out that night, I found Larry stabbed leaning on the Packard. I got him in the car, but I could see he was expiring. He was dead in three, maybe four blocks. So I got an idea."

"You decided to dump his corpse on me and get me off the case, tied up with cops or too busy to be in your way," I helped.

"Something like that. I lugged Larry's body to your place. Had a hell of a time conveying him up to your room without getting spotted," he said proudly.

"You did a fine job, but Larry wasn't dead."

Hanohyez looked into my eyes, which were probably in shadow. "I know when a guy is dead," he said dangerously.

"You put my knife into your brother-in-law, right back in the messy hole Tillman had made but he wasn't dead when you did it. When I got to my room, he was alive. He told me you killed him.

"That's enough horse crap, Peters," he squealed.

"No horse crap. I thought he was saying no. Yes. I figured he was trying to say Noyes. Hell, I was making it harder than it was. He was just trying to say your name, Hanohyez.

He thought you murdered him, and he may have been right."

"Maybe I made a faux pas," he said.

"Maybe your last big faux pas," I answered, watching the barrel of the .45 rise from my chest to my face. My .38 was already in his pocket, and my heart was trying to find a way out of my chest. I sighed, sagging my shoulders, trying to look resigned, smiled and went to one knee, throwing a right at Hanohyez's stomach. The bullet went where my head had been and a lot of air plushed out of Hanohyez, but he held onto the gun as he went back into the promenade railing and tried to level it at me as he gurgled for air.

I hesitated, unsure of whether to make a try for him or run like hell for the nearest cover. Cover promised the most hope. I got to my feet and ran. The second bullet cried past my head. When Hanohyez caught his breath, he would be shooting straight and painfully.

A third shot chucked splinters out of the cotton-candy stand I had ducked around. He had started stumbling after me, and he'd soon be running. His legs were big and heavy, but he had a lot of need and a gun on his side. I wondered how long it would take for someone to call the cops when they heard the gunshots. I wondered if anyone actually heard the shots. I wondered if the photograph on my office wall would go to my brother or my ex-wife if Hanohyez put a good one through my spine.

I had someplace to get to, but getting there was not a sure thing. A dash across an open walk brought me to the struts of a roller coaster. I climbed over the low wooden fence and went for the darkness of the steel framework. Over my shoulder I could see Hanohyez coming in my direction. He had spotted me.

On my knees in shadow I let myself pant, then took a few deep breaths and held the last one as I saw his big body, gun in hand, come over the small fence. He did the right thing. Instead of plunging into the darkness after me, he stood and waited till he caught his breath, and then he listened.

I had to breathe finally, and his head cocked in my direction. The fourth bullet hit a metal bar in front of my eyes and sent out a spark of light. I wasn't counting the bullets, waiting for them to run out. He didn't have a six-shooter and this wasn't a Western. Maybe I was counting to see how much beyond reason I was surviving.

Hanohyez was about twenty yards behind me when I vaulted the fence and found myself near a dip in the roller-coaster track. I could have gone over the other side and made a dash across an open square, where I'd be a great target, or I could climb up the track. If I made it to the first turn on the track and he followed me, I'd have a chance. I didn't figure him to be a climber. I scrambled up, grabbing chain and track, and got to the first curve as Hanohyez spotted me and sent a hasty shot in my direction. It dug into the wood near my shoulder with a sickly thunk.

If Hanohyez were a reasonable man, he wouldn't have followed me. He would have gone ahead of me on the ground and waited. I couldn't hide very well on top of a roller-coaster track. If he went ahead he could pluck me off. But he didn't know when company might come, and the straightest route seemed best. He came up the track. I could hear him cursing, but I also knew that to climb, he'd have to put the .45 in his holster. I peered back over the curve and saw him coming on. There was nothing to throw at him. I considered rolling myself down on him, but the chances of either of us surviving were small. So I went on, scrambling down a dip and climbing up an even higher incline than the first. Over my right shoulder I had a beautiful view of Santa Monica. The Douglas plant was belching fire from its chimneys to turn out planes. Over my left shoulder the moon sent out a white sheet over the ocean. Behind me, Hanohyez stood at the top of the lower incline and took careful aim in my direction.

This bullet tore hair and skin from my neck. It was the scratch of a wild witch and gave me a push over the top and down the other side.

I nearly lost my grip going down, and I didn't like the fact that I couldn't hear Hanohyez resolutely coming after me. Another idea must have entered his head, a good idea. When I got to the bottom of the dip, I was about a dozen feet from the ground. I hung over the side and let myself drop. I hit dirt, stumbled back and banged against a white picket fence designed to keep the curious away from danger.

My neck wound pulsed. I touched it and asked it to be patient for the sake of all my body parts and functions. Hanohyez wasn't in sight. I looked again and took off in the direction of the Dome Pier. He spotted me when I had almost made it across Pier Avenue. His footsteps echoed through the "Fun Zone" of concession booths and cafés, but he didn't shoot. He could see that I wasn't going for the street but heading for the ocean. Maybe he could even see that I was trapping myself.

My footsteps grew louder and joined my heart in "When the Saints Go Marching In" as I went on. I was tired, but there wasn't much further to go. At the end of the pier, I turned left on the walkway and moved more slowly. Behind me I could hear Hanohyez's heavier tramping on the wooden walk. I stopped at the railing and looked back as his footsteps grew louder. And then he turned the corner with his gun raised.

"Okay," I panted, standing in the shadow about thirty yards from him. "I quit. Just make it as painless as possible."

Hanohyez walked forward, gun out slowly. "Like hell," he said.

"One last question," I said, stepping out into the light. "Did you enjoy killing Lombardi or Tillman? How about Larry?"

"I rubbed them out because I had to. It's my vocation. I ain't no nut who likes killing. But I'll make an exception in your case."

The gun was leveled at my chest, and the shot was loud and close, a crack and a boom like a bullwhip.

Hanohyez looked at his gun and then looked at me and said, "I'm terminated." He put the gun back in his holster and toppled forward like Jimmy Cagney at the end of *Public Enemy*. I imagined the splinters hitting his face, and I felt sick.

Phil stepped out of the shadows where I had been and moved down the walkway with his gun drawn and extended. Seidman moved to the other side of the railing, behind me, with his gun out. They were both pointing the weapons at the prone Hanohyez, who wasn't quite dead. They were taking no chances. Both of them and I had seen more than one Lazarus rise from the dead to take another shot at an unwary cop.

Seidman moved ahead and kicked Hanohyez with his toe while Phil covered him. Hanohyez groaned.

"You heard?" I said, hearing the distant scream of the mad gull of Ocean Park.

"We heard," said Seidman. "Full confession."

I had asked Jeremy Butler to call Phil and have him hide at the corner of the pier while I brought the killer to him for a confession. Hanohyez had had other ideas, however, and those other ideas had almost cost me my plan and my life.

Phil put his pistol away and strode back toward me.

"You bagged another bad guy," I said, waving. Phil swayed before my eyes, moonlight behind him. My vision was hazy, and he seemed to rise slowly from the pier like Harry Blackstone's assistant.

"All a joke to you," he said, standing in front of me. I must have grinned because he put a broad hand on my neck to squeeze or shake a little brotherly sense into me, but his hand felt blood and came away quickly.

"You're hurt," he said, grabbing my arm.

"Hell," I laughed, "it takes a silver bullet to kill me."

When I woke up a few hours later with Koko the Clown urging me off the air mattress and into the ocean, a rush of white made me wince and I closed my eyes again. I opened them slowly and realized I was in a Los Angeles County hospital.

Phil was leaning against the wall with his arms folded. He ran his hand through his hair, sighed and shook his head. "At least this time, no one used your head for a coconut," he said.

I sat up, feeling dizzy. My neck was stiff and I reached for it. A bandage held it in place.

"Keep your hands off," Phil said, stepping forward to whack my hand away. I almost fell off the table.

"Marco?" I said.

"Still alive," said Phil.

"And what happened to Fargo and Gelhorn?" I said, feeling sick to my stomach.

"Let them go," he said.

"Let them go?"

"I can't hold them if there are no charges. You want to place charges? You think charges from you will hold up?" Phil was getting angry again, and I was in no condition to deal with his fists.

"What about Cooper and Hemingway?" I tried. "They wouldn't press charges?"

"No," he said. "Cooper said as far as he was concerned, it was all over, and he didn't want any publicity. Had to let them go, but I had a nice talk with Gelhorn before he saw the door."

Phil's eyes glinted with satisfaction, and I imagined Gelhorn's little talk with him. It would be a talk that would have made Tony Galento want to stay away from further discussion.

“We’ve got no charges on you,” Phil said, keeping his hands folded as I stood on wobbly legs. “You can’t drive. Come back to my place. Ruth wants to be sure you’re all right.”

I didn’t argue. To argue meant I might win. Then I’d have to get a ride to Ocean Park, drive back to Hollywood and face the possibility of Mrs. Plaut before I could make it to bed. It was easier to nod and let Phil lead the way to his car.

We didn’t talk on the way through Laurel Canyon and into North Hollywood. I kept dozing and clutched the bottle of white pills the nurse had given me for pain. Phil had told me that my .38 would be returned after a full investigation. I was in no hurry to get it back.

When we got to his house, we woke up Ruth and my nephews Dave and Nate. They thanked me for Babe Ruth’s autograph and admired my wound. I almost told them their old man had drilled a bad guy, but I changed my mind. I had said too many wrong things in front of them in the past. The noise of a two A.M. family get-together woke the baby, Lucy, who wondered why I had a diaper on my neck.

“He peed on his neck,” said Dave, giggling. Nate hit him, and Phil rapped Nate on the head.

Ruth, looking thin, her hair in a puffy pink bag, hugged herself against the cold that wasn’t there and offered me something to drink. Before I could get the drink she went for, I was asleep in a chair.

On Sunday morning I woke up, unable to move my neck. Phil was gone, on duty. Ruth and the kids had waited around to be sure I was alive before they went to Ruth’s mother in Pasadena for the day.

“How come you always get blasted, Uncle Tobe?” asked Nate.

“You should see the other guy?” countered Dave.

I was glad they didn’t see the other guy. They might be

able to sleep a few more nights without the things that had crept into my dreams.

We good-byed for about five minutes, and Lucy managed to sneak up behind me and wallop me with the padlock from Dave's bike. She laughed. I declined breakfast from Ruth, waved them away, took a pain pill, called a Yellow Cab and sat rigid-necked all the way to Ocean Park.

Receipt in hand from the cab, I drove slowly to the Farraday Building, trying to ignore the parking ticket that clung to my windshield wiper. I hoped the wind would grab it and take it for a ride. I wanted to ignore it.

There wasn't much traffic on Hoover. I parked near the office and went in.

Somewhere in the heights or depths of the building, someone was drunkenly singing "Side by Side." By the time I got to my office, the double-echoed voice had gone through the song twice and was bellowing "Maybe we're ragged and funny."

The door was locked and I let myself in. Sunday or no, my case was closed, and I had a bill to make out. I sat in my office listening to a guy with a sugar voice read the funny papers on the radio while I transferred costs from my notebook to my bill. Should I charge Cooper for bullets? Yes. How about the cost of the *High Midnight* script? Why not? I pulled the script from my desk drawer and added the cost of hot dogs, a shirt, tacos, gas, a motel bill, sundry items and emergency medical treatment.

I didn't hear the door to the outer office open. I was having enough trouble juggling my accounts and trying to find out from the guy reading the funnies if Tiny Tim was going to get out of the bottle he was trapped in.

When my door opened, I was aware of two bodies standing in it but I couldn't place the faces for an instant. That was because I had never seen them in suits before; only in white smocks at Lombardi's.

"No office hours on Sunday," I said, leaning back to look at them since I couldn't lift my head. "Come back to-morrow."

Steve didn't answer and Al stepped to one side of the door. Their hands were in their pockets.

"You don't know when to give up, do you?" Steve said.

"Come on," I said wearily. "I didn't kill Lombardi. Hanohyez did. He came here from Chicago to kill Lombardi. He was sent. If he hadn't got nailed by the cops last night, he'd probably be out today mopping up loose ends, like you two."

"It won't do," Steve said, hesitating.

"It won't do what?" I said. "Be my guest." I picked up the phone and handed it to him. "Call Chicago or New York or wherever you call and take a chance with your life. You can either say Lombardi's dead and you're going to find who did it and settle the score, or you can say Hanohyez got killed but you helped him dump Lombardi before he went. Try it. You tell the first tale and I give you a week to ten days. You tell the second tale and you inherit a sausage factory."

I gave him the phone. "I'll even give you the nickels," I said.

Steve looked at Al, who looked at Steve, who looked at me.

"We're going to think about it," he said. "If you turned us wrong on this, we'll be back."

"Why not kill him just to be sure?" Al tried. I turned my body toward him so I could see him and show my an-noyance.

"We're not killing him if we don't have to. The less killing you do, the fewer raps can come back to haunt you," Steve said, waving Al out the door. Al gave me a sneer and went for the outer office.

Steve stayed behind for a few seconds to stare me down. It was hard to keep my eyes on him without hurting my neck, but it was his game. In thirty seconds he had had enough and went out, closing the door behind him. I popped a pain pill, touched my neck carefully and put my hand over my mouth. In a few minutes I was ready to get back to my bill. Twenty minutes later I had it finished and ready for delivery.

I called the number Cooper had given me, not expecting an answer. I imagined Hemingway and Cooper back in the hills firing madly at scampering, oinking wild pigs that Luís Felípe Castelli was flushing out with his ax. Between the shots the good old boys were swapping lies about women.

I was wrong. Cooper answered. "Thought you might be calling," he said. "Can I meet you someplace?"

"I can come over there," I said, "but if you feel like a Sunday out, you can come to my office. I've had a little scratch."

I gave him directions to the Farraday and told him to follow the sound of the drunk singing "Side by Side." Hell, since I was pushing, I asked him to bring me a sandwich and a Pepsi. He gave me a clipped yes and hung up.

Maybe the pills got to me or the pain or the image of Hanohyez lying on the pier, but I found myself passing the time by arguing with a Sunday-morning radio Evangelist who kept telling me where my soul was going if I didn't straighten up. I stopped talking when I heard the outer door open and Cooper's voice.

"Peters?" he said.

"In here," I answered, and he followed my voice into the small office. He had a bag in hand and a Coke. I was sure I had said Pepsi, but this was no time for a culinary argument.

Cooper looked ready to meet royalty. He wore a dark suit with wide lapels and dark stripes. A little handkerchief peeked out of his left breast pocket.

"Have a seat," I said, holding the package up to remove a sandwich.

He sat and put his hands on his knees. "What happened to you?" he said.

I told him as I ate, and then I countered, "Why didn't you let the cops hold Fargo and Gelhorn?"

Cooper shrugged. "Why? It's all over, isn't it? Besides, Fargo and Gelhorn know about Luís. Papa and I decided to call it square. Big cop with gray hair and mean eyes said he'd talk to them and show them the error of their ways."

I handed Cooper my bill, and he dug into his pocket, pulled out a wallet and counted off four one-hundred-dollar bills.

"You did swell," he said. "I wish I could have helped you more."

"My job," I said. "You stick to acting and I'll stick to getting my head pummeled."

"It's a deal," he smiled. He wanted to go, and I guess I wanted him to go, but we didn't know quite how to end it. I asked him a question about his suit, and he told me tales of learning how to dress from some countess in Europe.

"I think Papa's sorry about you and him not hitting it off," Cooper said, standing.

"I never met your old man," I said, trying not to count the money again in front of him.

"No," he laughed, "Hemingway–friends call him Papa. I think there's too much of what he admires in you. It challenged him. Next step is for him to declare undying friendship."

"You are a philosopher, Coop," I said, getting up and putting out my hand. He took it firmly.

"You know," he said, "that *High Midnight* script isn't bad at all." He pointed at the script on my desk. "Title's good. Too bad."

We walked to the door and into the hall, where he told me I didn't have to go down with him.

"See you around," he said, waving at me.

"See you around," I said, waving back. All he needed was a horse and some reasonable background music, but there was no horse, only the drunk who had gone from "Side by Side" to "We're in the Money."

I closed up, packed my money and went home. Gunther was there, and I invited him out for Sunday dinner. It took Gunther twenty minutes to dress, though he had already looked ready for a banquet when I walked in.

Over egg foo yung and pressed duck at Jee Gong Law's on Alameda, Gunther displayed his knowledge of Chinese and I ate, stiff-necked and with wild abandon. We toasted Gary Cooper, Luís Felípe Castelli, Ernest Hemingway and Eleanor Roosevelt.

Something had ended, and I had that nagging fear that nothing else was ready to begin. I washed away visions of filling in for Jack Ellis at the Ocean Palms with tea, beer and talk.

"I think it is now time to go home," Gunther said finally.

I was about to argue with him, but realized he was right. I called for the check, overtipped and wondered on the way home if Mrs. Plaut would take kindly to my having a dog—maybe a dog who looked like my old beagle Kaiser Wilhelm.

CHAPTER THIRTEEN

Monday morning made me no great promises. In fact, it said, "This is the way the world ends. Take it or leave it." My neck was feeling better, though I had no plans for getting rid of the bandage till I'd milked a few more hours of sympathy from the wound. The Sunday *Los Angeles Times* sat unread on my table. The headlines were enough to keep me from trespassing on the possible horrors inside. If the *Times* was right, the war must be about over and we were about to lose.

Even with more than four hundred dollars in my pocket, I would have felt better with some hope that a job might be waiting for me. The only thing going for me was the fact that I had gone through a case without a major back problem. I could have felt sorry for myself and slept if the sun weren't so bright. I had no curtains and a low tolerance for the light of the sun.

I treated myself to three cereals mixed together in my salad bowl: Wheaties, Puffed Rice and Bran Flakes. I put too much sugar on the pile and a little milk. The hell with it.

Mrs. Plaut wasn't prowling around when I went out, but

she had left more chapters of her family history for me. With her treasures removed from my room and no corpses in evidence, she was ready to deal with me again as a literary critic and household-pest exterminator. By my conservative estimate, Mrs. Plaut's book now totaled over two thousand pages, neatly hand-printed.

Things were no better when I got to the Buick. It had heard the war news and was feeling sorry for itself. All the way downtown the car screamed sadly. By the time I drove it in to No-neck Arnie the mechanic, the car was crying like an abandoned cat.

Arnie gave it a stern look and ignored me. He took the keys and told me he'd call when he had anything to call about, providing I left him with a deposit. I forked over twenty bucks, which disappeared into his overalls, and left.

No one was waiting to kill me or beat me to a pulp in the lobby of the Farraday Building. On the second-floor landing I found Jeremy Butler running his fingers along the outside of the door to a baby photographer's office.

"Maybe termites," he said with concern, and then turned to look at me.

I told my tale, thanked him for his help and accepted sympathy for the wounds taken in the line of duty.

"Sometimes I think if I were twenty, thirty years younger," he said, "I'd join the army and go out and wring some Nazi necks. Then sometimes I think I'm lucky I'm not twenty, thirty years younger, and that makes me feel ashamed. You know?"

"Right," I agreed. It was a morning for agreeing with people who felt sorry for themselves.

"So," sighed Jeremy, taking a last look at the door before going down the stairs, "I'll just write a poem about it and that will make me feel guilty. I wish there were a bum or two to throw out."

He went down the stairs and got lost below me. I hoped he found a bum or two. If I had the time, and I probably did, I could go pay a few bucks to have some rummy infest the Farraday to keep Jeremy's mind off the war.

Shelly was sitting in the dental chair when I came in. The script to *High Midnight* was open in his lap and his eyes, behind thick lenses, were inches from the page. He turned a page near the end and looked up. "Be with you in a minute," he said.

"It's me, Shel, Toby."

"What're you wearing a scarf for?" he asked, returning to the manuscript. "It's up to 70 degrees out there. Don't you know it's anti-California to wear a scarf? It's never cold enough here to wear a scarf even when it's cold enough here to wear a scarf."

"I'm not wearing a scarf," I said. "I was shot in the neck Saturday night."

Without taking his eyes from the page, Shelly went on. "Take my advice and stay home on Saturday nights. Wild people, wild crowds out there. War scare. It's hurting business, too. People don't want to take care of their teeth if they think they won't have their heads in a few months. At least some people. On the other hand, some people want to look their best if they know they're going. However, the ones who don't care . . ."

"Forget it, Shel," I said.

He shrugged and turned the last page of the script.

"Well?" I asked, going for the coffee. "How do you like it?"

"Ah," he said, tapping the script with his hand and sitting up in the chair. "Not bad, but it could be better. Some good ideas."

He accepted a cup of black liquid, touched his stubbly chin, shifted his cigar and said, "First of all, it should be a lot simpler. The way I see it, the old sheriff isn't a killer. He's tired, and he's all set to retire, leave town with his pal the dentist."

"Dentist?" I said, trying to drink the coffee.

"Doc Holliday was a dentist," said Shelly with pride. "Sheriff and the dentist are going to leave town, retire together. Town gives them a big sendoff. Then they find that a gang of guys the sheriff put in jail are free and coming to shoot it out that very day. Sheriff tries to gather the townspeople to help him. They all give excuses, except the dentist. Together the sheriff and the dentist face the gang, and in the last scene they leave town, and the sheriff, who's been wounded in the neck, throws down his badge. Huh, how about that for a story?"

"No good," I said. "Americans don't want to see stories during the war about people not wanting to help each other to fight off the bad guys."

"Maybe you're right," said Shelly. "Maybe I'm a man ahead of his time."

"You are indeed a man of many parts, Shel," I agreed, coming down to something solid at the bottom of my cup.

"The title has to go," said Shelly. "*High Midnight* sounds like a Boris Karloff. I think they should call it *High—*"

"Forget it, Shel," I said, looking down into the cup. "What the hell is this?"

"Frog," said Sheldon Minck, leaning back to dream about his script. "Porcelain. Used to do that back in the colonial days. You know, have frogs, other stuff at the bottom. Dentist wrote an article about making them as novelties when business is slow. Good gag, huh?"

A patient walked in, the reluctant Mr. Stange, who took one step back for every one he took forward.

"Wasn't going to come back," he said, "but it hurts like chicken hell."

"A powerful image," said Shelly, getting out of the chair and pointing to it to show Mr. Stange the way. "Enter and be sanctified."

Mr. Stange went to the chair and got in, ready for another fearful trip. I had no intention of watching.

"Any calls?" I said as Shelly began to hum and rub his hands together as he looked for a tool or two in the rubble. He scratched his little finger pensively as he mumbled, "Calls, calls. Yes, you had a call, but it was nothing, just some clown playing a joke. You've picked up a lot of cuckoos in your line, let me tell you. Mildred thinks—"

"I know," I said. "What was the message?"

"On your desk." With that Shel shrugged and gave up his search for the elusive proper tool. He settled for second or third best, a long thing with a pincer at the end, which he cleaned by blowing on it and rubbing it against his soiled smock.

"When duty calls, a Minck will always respond."

I left and closed my office door behind me, hoping it would drown out some of the more terrible sounds from Mr. Stange and some of the more gleeful ones of Sheldon P. Minck. It was somewhat effective, but it could have been better.

Among the pile of bills, mailers for a few dozen products to make me a more patriotic citizen and a handbill telling me to save all my chicken fat so it could be turned into explosives by my local butcher, I found the scrawled message Shelly had taken:

> Guy called. Sounded funny. Said someone had electrocuted an elephant. I told him someone else had fried an eel. Guy on the phone said, someone had killed the elephant and I think we're in danger. Guy said his name was Emmett Kelly, and you should come to San

Diego right away and meet him with the Ringling Brothers Circus. I told him you'd be there in a few hours riding on your pet lion. Ha. Ha.

I put the note in my coat pocket, shoveled the mail and bills into my bulging top drawers and went into the outer office.

"I may not be back for a few days," I told Shelly and Mr. Stange. I was feeling pretty good. In fact, I was feeling damned good. It sounded strange, but it didn't have the ring of a gag. I could smell a gag as far away as I could smell Shelly Minck.

"Where are you going?" asked Shelly, his eyes in Mr. Stange's gummy mouth.

"San Diego, to see who killed an elephant," I said with a foolish grin.

"Waste of time," said Shelly. "I tell you, it's just some clown."